# FLIGHT OF A WILD HEART

## HEARTS OF ROARING FORK VALLEY

SARA BLACKARD

INKED HEART PRESS, LLC

Copyright © 2023 by Sara Blackard

All rights reserved.

No part of this book may be reproduced in any form or by any electronic or mechanical means, including information storage and retrieval systems, without written permission from the author, except for the use of brief quotations in a book review.

# CHAPTER 1

*Roaring Fork Valley, Colorado, 1880*

Robert Sweeney leaned against a boulder, drinking his coffee as the clear creek gurgled by. The birds twittered happily in the shrubs and trees, singing away the last remnants of summer. All around him leaves changed to different shades of green, gold, orange, and brown. The breeze carried the scent of new beginnings in the crisp, tangy smell of autumn.

Most people considered spring the symbol of new life. To Robert, autumn would forever remind him of when he finally gained control of his life. He bowed his head and thanked Jesus for the second chance. The weight of that responsibility settled heavily on his bent shoulders and lowered head. Robert didn't care. His wide shoulders were strong enough to carry the burden of his duty to God. He would carry the weight of the world if it meant he lived out a life worth living.

He raised his head and surveyed the land around him. His land. Relief filled his lungs and sprung wells from his eyes. He quickly dashed the moisture away. He wondered if he let the dam of emotions break, would he ever be able to wall it back up? He wasn't sure, so he closed his eyes, took a deep breath, and found the control that had gotten him through hell and back.

Guilt quickly replaced the sense of relief. Robert sighed. He should've known the pleasant feeling wouldn't last. The last two years had chiseled just about every good feeling out of him.

He huffed as he rubbed the back of his neck. His entire life had done that. Not that it mattered now. The consequences of his choices would always be with him. At least now he had the hope of heaven and a roadmap of the path to get there. All he had to do was stay the course, keep everything tightly in control, and he'd make it.

He gazed up at Mount Sopris where it towered in the distance. *I will lift up mine eyes unto the hills, from whence cometh my help.* He glanced at the Bible that sat upon the boulder he had been leaning against. The truth of that verse settled his mind. God had helped him. When his brother Linc had been set on kidnapping Viola to claim her as his own, God had given Robert the courage to tell his brother no and keep his younger brother, William, from running off with Linc.

After Linc no longer had control over Robert, God had shown him the sack of coins Linc had hidden in his bedroll. Robert had no clue who Linc stole the money from and felt guilty about not being able to return it. It also angered Robert as all get-out that Linc couldn't see past his greed to appreciate what he already had. Robert had taken those coins and set off to find a new way of life.

Robert rinsed out his coffee mug in the stream,

grabbed his Bible, and headed to the cabin. He couldn't believe he had gotten the cabin up before winter set in. It would've been easier if William had been able to pitch in.

Robert swallowed the grief that closed off his throat. He had known William needed help, that something in his brain had cracked. Robert wanted to blame Linc and his abuse of the boy, but he couldn't lie to himself or God. If he would've taken William away and not allowed Linc to take out his anger on William, the sweet boy that had raced up to Robert as a child back east wouldn't have ended up a crazed man with a knife in his chest. After Robert had buried William in the mountains that had claimed half his family, he'd headed to Leadville, hoping to find work for the winter and figure out what he was supposed to do next. When news of the Utes being rounded up that next spring hit, he took off for the Roaring Fork.

Before Linc had died, he'd always made them check out the valley, in between his stalking the Thomas family. He swore if they kept coming back to the area and the surrounding mountains, they'd someday find a miner, and they could jump his claim. Of course, Linc had never been willing to find a claim of his own, especially when he could steal someone else's.

However, Robert had looked upon the vast valley and found land perfect for farming. When the government ripped the lands back from the Utes, he had seen his future. One he'd till and form from the land. He had the ten dollars needed to claim the homestead as soon as a land office opened up close, and enough coins left to get him through the next winter and spring. Then he planned to plant enough food, not only for himself, but also to supply the mines he figured would crop up by next spring.

A grin stole up his face as he approached the cabin. He rubbed his cheek at the unfamiliar tug and decided to let it stay. It felt right that one would grin like a fool when freedom had been granted. The cabin walls were six-feet tall with the purlin peak for the roof another six-feet up. Robert meant to build it much shorter, but with each row of logs he stacked, he realized he didn't want to spend his life stooped in discomfort any longer.

He'd cut one small window in the side wall he planned to cover with furs once the real cold set in. Then, he had stacked the fireplace and chimney with rocks from the creek outside. It warmed the cabin up quite nicely, which made him thankful he wouldn't freeze through another winter.

The handmade cottonwood shingles had taken the longest to get on. The meticulous work of roofing may have been tedious for most, but he found it soothing. His attention to detail proved watertight through the storms that passed the last week.

He'd chinked between the logs with the pretty red clay found in the area and thought it gave the cabin a nice decorative look. He snorted at himself. Who was he kidding? It was a simple, one-room cabin with nothing fancy to it, but it was his. It represented a life of stability he'd staked claim to for himself.

Robert swung the homemade door open and stomped into the cabin. The thick walls muted the singing of the birds, and quiet enveloped him. He set his mug on the shelf next to his one and only plate, rubbing his hand on the smooth wood before turning. Would the loneliness of not having his family near break his mind like William's had? Was his family destined for madness?

Pa had beat into the boys that family stuck together, no matter what. Robert and Linc had understood that message to mean different things. Linc had spent his days growing up trying to live up to their pa's depravity. That left Robert to take care of the family, though he was two years younger than Linc.

As a child, Robert found food in the alleys and gardens back home, while his pa drank and gambled away any money he made working and his ma survived the atrocities Pa put her through. How she kept her faith in God with that monster of a husband was beyond Robert's comprehension. He now thanked God every day she did, because her faith eventually saved him from the worst of his family's sins. He hadn't wanted her to suffer more, so he dug through trash and stole vegetables from gardens to feed everyone. A pat on the cheek and a sorrowful smile was all the encouragement he had needed to make sure his ma had food, though the act of stealing always made his stomach hurt.

The fear of solitude was the reason he'd stayed with Linc after their ma died. He always told himself he stayed to take care of his family, but that was a bald-faced lie. His brothers were all he had in the world, were his responsibility for most of his life. He had been so plumb worried the loneliness would tear at him that he'd followed Linc to the very edge of the pit to hell. Robert should've dealt with the loneliness, because the scars of who he had become would terrorize him until the day he died.

Sparrow made her way from Orlando and Samara Thomas's homestead toward her home next to the Yampah. Talk in her village over the winter that the government might force them to move had driven her up the mountain to visit her cousin's sweet baby, Zachary, possibly for the last time. After the horrible catastrophe at the White River Agency the fall before, her band knew their life on their ancestral grounds would end sooner than later. Some still hoped that Chief Ouray could convince the government to keep their treaty. After what Sparrow witnessed with the death of Meeker and the other workers, hope hadn't sprouted up in her heart.

She only meant to visit with the Thomas family for a week or two. Their last visit had been so full of desperation and sorrow that she needed to have happy memories of the adorable red-haired baby who had stolen her heart and made her long for a child of her own. That was a longing she'd better push aside.

When she arrived, the love that saturated the Thomas's mountain homestead filled her up and slowed down time. Instead of visiting for a few weeks, three months passed before she forced herself to head down the mountain back to her band. More like the Lord told her it was time to go, because she doubted she would have left without divine prodding.

Zachary had grown into such a big baby with his wild red hair that stuck out in all directions and his dark brown eyes that looked deep into her soul. They'd spent many hours scouting the area for herbs and mushrooms, chatting back and forth. She'd sung him Ute lullabies as he drank his bottle and fell asleep in her arms. She'd been selfish with her time with him, but Samara and Orlando sensed her need and indulged her. She didn't quite understand the yearning herself. Leaving had been hard, but she trusted God's guidance and timing.

Sparrow rejoiced in the happiness Orlando and Samara found in each other. She knew how the love of a spouse could bring healing. She smiled wistfully and leaned her head back to allow the sun to warm her face. The gentle sway of the horse's gait lulled her to a distant past she'd lingered on more in the last three months than she had in the last four years.

Her late husband's face appeared in the darkness of her closed eyes. His blond hair hanging haphazardly across his forehead and his blue eyes intent upon her. She opened her eyes and wiped the tear that raced down her cheek. Theirs had been a love no one expected.

John came to Chief Ouray's band to learn the history of the Utes firsthand. He had been a reporter sent to travel with the military and had witnessed the hardships many tribes were put through. Chief Ouray's willingness to find peace for his people encouraged John. He had hoped if he could report the history of the Ute people, show the rest of the nation the love and devotion they had for each other, maybe there would be a change in the way the tribes of the west were treated.

Sparrow, adopted into the home of her uncle Chief Ouray when her family was killed, had listened to Ouray and John talk for hours about the future of the Ute people. John's desire to find common ground fascinated her and filled her with dreams of a peaceful future. She had often lain on her pallet at night, wondering what would drive a man with no connection to any tribe, whose family prospered in the steel industry back east, to leave everything to champion a people he didn't even know. She'd boldly asked him one night while they talked in Ouray's adobe home.

John had looked her straight in the eye, his face ablaze with fierce determination. "The Lord told me in a dream that my future waited here. We just fought a brutal war under the belief that all men, no matter the color of your skin, are created equal under the eyes of God and our nation. Why are the Indians any different? With God's help, I plan on showing that the Utes and other tribes have a right to land just as much as the other citizens of this great country do."

John's passion had flamed a desire she'd thought long buried with her family. She and John had spent many nights and long days talking about God and His calling for them in life. When they married, John had claimed God had much more than he had ever imagined waiting for him in the arid mountain desert of the Colorado territory. Their love had filled the teepee and floated out to the others in their band, a hope that the whites and Utes might live beside each other like the Mexicans and Apaches did with the Utes.

Sparrow pulled her horse Lightning to a stop and looked absentmindedly across the Grand River. The love she and John had shared had crashed and tumbled away like the waters of the mighty river when sickness fell upon the village. Not only did it take John like a thief at night but left her swollen womb empty in its wake. She had questioned why God could be so cruel to allow her to stay and take everything from her again.

Trapper Dan, a longtime friend of the Utes and unofficial missionary, had come to her when her grief threatened to overwhelm her and sat for long hours praying over her. He had told her of his love's death, how he too had questioned God. While he explained he didn't know why God took the lives of those they loved, Trapper Dan knew within his spirit there was a reason for Sparrow's survival. Not to live in pain and sorrow, but for a heavenly purpose beyond this earth. His prayers had shaken her out of her mire.

God brought purpose and strength out of the ashes of grief. Hadn't that been proven in Chief Ouray's influence for the band as well as the strong love he shared with his second wife, Chipeta?

While another love like Sparrow and John's was impossible for her, she grabbed onto the hope of John's mission and worked hard to see his writings published. Change for the Utes was inevitable. Sparrow prayed she could be a beacon for her people, bringing the hope of Jesus Christ's love to them like John had to her.

Lightning nickered and drew her attention to her surroundings. Her face relaxed in contentment as she sent another prayer up to the heavens, thanking God for giving her grief a purpose and lessening its hold on her heart. She clicked the horse forward and allowed the Grand River to wash away the last of her sadness as they swam across. If she was to be of any use to her people, she must be strong in the Lord. The stirring in her spirit warned her that her people would need His hope in the months and years to come.

## CHAPTER 2

Sparrow pulled up short when she emerged from the canyon into the Yampah Valley. Smoke billowed from a new cabin nestled between large cottonwoods that lined the river's edge. What brave soul would build a cabin on Ute land so defiantly against the treaty the white government had established with Chief Ouray? She tore her eyes from the cabin across the river and scanned the valley. Her chest tightened at the absence of teepees that normally dotted the area.

"Good hunting must be up valley still," she whispered to herself, patting Lightning's neck to calm herself more than the horse. "Come. We will find them."

Keeping to the mountains that loomed in the west so she didn't draw the attention of the squatters, Sparrow worked her way up the valley. The farther she travelled, the quicker her mind raced that all was not right. She stuck to the trees and brush as she searched for her band. When she reached where the Roaring Fork River connected with what the whites had called the Frying Pan

FLIGHT OF A WILD HEART

Creek, she jerked Lightning to a halt. White tents filled the land like daisies in spring where teepees should be.

"Well, look what we have here, boys." The deep voice raised the hairs on Sparrow's neck. "I think we've caught ourselves a horse thief."

All feeling rushed from Sparrow's body, leaving her lightheaded as she turned and peered into a face whose toothy smile and fancy clothes countered his sinister tone of voice. She tensed as other men eased their horses out of the bushes, a contrast to the first man in their filthy clothes and unkempt hair. All held the stench of unwashed bodies and trouble.

"Whatcha gonna do with her, Sterling?" A shorter man licked his lips as he stared at her in anticipation. His skinny arms adjusted the misshapen, dirty red hat squashed upon his head.

The question kicked Sparrow's heart into galloping like a thousand horses across the arid desert. Her eyes darted from one man to another. There were too many. She'd never be able to get away, even though her horse was as quick as her name. Sparrow steeled her spine and pulled her shoulders back.

Lifting a prayer of protection upward, she stared the leader in the eye. "I am no horse thief."

The man, Sterling, chuckled as he shook his head and leaned on his saddle horn. "Did you hear that, boys? The savage says she's not a horse thief." He sneered as the other men laughed. "Why don't we let the good folks of Fryingpan Town decide the truth to her statement?"

At the smattering of tents being referred to by name, her body chilled like a snowmelt creek. How could the government have possibly moved her people so soon? The band had assumed they had at least one more winter until the government forced them to leave. She should've stayed instead of indulging in her selfish whim. Who knew the pain her people endured without her to offer comfort? And what misery awaited her at the hands of a vengeful crowd?

The leader pulled his gun from his holster and pointed it at her. The others followed suit. Sparrow stared Sterling down, willing her fear not to show.

"Get down off your horse, nice and slow like. If you go for that bow of yours, I'll put a bullet through your horse's flank quicker than you can say Jack dandy." Sterling's eyes turned cold as sleet as he waved his gun at her to dismount.

Sparrow swung her leg over the rump of Lightning, nice and slow, not willing to give these men any more reason to shoot. Maybe that would be a more merciful way to go than what she could only imagine was ahead of her. Sterling motioned to one of the other men, and the man eased forward and reached for Lightning's reins. The horse reared up, slashing her hooves at the man.

"Whoa!" the man yelled, backing up and pointing his gun at Lightning's head.

While all the men started hollering like scared marmots, Sparrow quickly stepped between the man and Lightning, holding her hands up and shushing the horse like a baby. The horse settled but snorted her disgust into the air. Sparrow agreed with her horse. These men were revolting.

"Squaw, you lead that beast of yours." Sterling threw the derogatory term at her, and Sparrow bristled.

She rubbed Lightning on the nose one last time and

turned to the tent town, following behind Sterling who led the way. Her feet grew heavier the closer she got. The weight tempted her to glance down to see if clay had hardened upon her moccasins. With each step she took, the men's jeers battered her ears until she wished she could cover them and cower.

She wouldn't satisfy them by groveling or trembling before them. She would stand tall and strong as the pine, knowing that the God of David stood by her side. Though she was small like the shepherd of the Bible, and her enemy was huge, God had not changed.

As they drew near the tents, men started gathering, hollering to Sterling. Sterling rode his horse through the crowd, smiling left and right like a returning soldier from a victory. Sparrow followed, Lightning plodding behind her.

Sparrow never took her eyes off Sterling's back. Never bowed her head in shame. When a good-size crowd formed, Sterling stopped his horse and held up his hand for silence.

Once the crowd quieted, Sterling spoke proudly to the men. "Gentlemen, I've had the unfortunate pleasure of running into a savage scout slinking through the woods."

An uproar rose from the crowd as something pelted her skirt. Sparrow stared straight forward over the heads of the men to the mountains beyond, clenching and unclenching her fists at her side. *My help cometh from the hills. My help cometh from the hills.*

"Not only did I catch her scouting for the best way to attack our fair town, but I'm convinced she's a horse thief at that." Sterling motioned toward Lightning. "No savage has a mount as fine as that after the army came through here and rounded them up."

Sparrow thought Sterling's argument ridiculous. Anyone with knowledge of the Ute people would never consider her a scout or question the quality of their mounts. However, the increased fervor of the crowd slicked her hands with sweat and caught her breath in her throat. Was there no one in this town that would stand up for her?

"What are we going to do with her?" someone from the crowd hollered.

"Well, I'll tell you what I have planned for this little morsel." Sterling held up his hands as if to savor the anticipation of the moment, making the crowd wait as he paused for effect. "I know some of y'all like to get a little wild sometimes, so I'm adding her to my girls down in the cribs. Highest bidder gets first go of her."

Sparrow shook her head as she backed up from the men whose eyes had turned from anger to lust in a split second. Her heart raced as she closed her eyes to the onslaught.

She tilted her head back in prayer, the heat of the sun on her face the only comfort as her body shuddered in terror. A shadow blocked the sun, causing her eyes to pop open. A man the size of Goliath towered beside her, his face grim and harsh. She'd been wrong. With her knees knocking so hard she feared she'd collapse, she was nothing like the brave David of old.

THE LOUD RUMBLING of a crowd drew Robert's attention as he entered Fryingpan Town. He rarely ventured there, preferring the solitude of his homestead to the rowdiness of the tent community. It reminded him too much of his past to want to spend any time chattering like magpies with the locals.

Robert froze as he took in the crowd surrounding a lone Ute woman. She stood there, her tiny stature strong and her head held high like a warrior princess. How could one so little have such bravery?

His eyes blinked rapidly as he tried to understand what he was seeing. The ringmaster of this circus claimed the woman was a horse thief, causing an uproar to rage through the already rowdy and bored men. Robert's blood ran hot at the obvious lie and manipulation. Anyone with a decent set of eyes could see the horse was clearly hers. He leaned forward to dismount to try and diffuse the mob.

The man causing the ruckus turned to survey the crowd. Sterling Fitzgerald. The heat of Robert's blood froze, and he paused next to his horse. He hadn't seen Sterling since he and his brothers had left their hometown back east. It appeared Sterling had done well for himself, if his dandy suit and fancy saddle spoke the truth.

Robert bent over the saddle horn, trying to stop the memories spinning in his head and making him lightheaded. Sterling had witnessed Robert's pa beating a man to death in an alley, an event Robert had the misfortune of seeing as well. Sterling had intimidated Robert with the act for months, forcing him to keep quiet when Robert had caught Sterling taking advantage of a young woman. Robert had wanted to intervene, but the fear of what Sterling would do to his family had Robert turning and rushing off. The shame of his cowardice still churned his gut. When his pa was shot in a gambling dispute, and his ma died from her sickness shortly after, Robert had been all too ready to leave the city and head west.

He inhaled deeply and pulled his shoulders back. He was no longer the scrawny young man, boy really, with the heavy responsibility of family hanging around his neck. He had grown eight inches and bulked on some muscle since the last time he'd seen Sterling. So why did he hold back?

Sterling calmed the crowd down for his next pronouncement, sick satisfaction clear upon his face. The petite warrior princess shook her head at what Sterling intended. Robert ground his teeth, swung from his horse, and stomped through the crowd. He couldn't allow Sterling to ruin another woman's life. Sterling no longer had any power over Robert, and if he did, Robert would just deal with the consequences of his sins. No woman, Ute or not, deserved what Sterling had planned.

Robert pushed his way through the throng. Men let him pass with one look at his size. He took a deep breath to fortify himself and stepped up next to the woman. Now that he was close, he saw her trembling like a leaf with her eyes closed and head tipped to the sky. Robert kept his gaze glued to Sterling but saw her almond-shaped eyes pop open wide and stare up at Robert. He motioned with his hand to her, hoping to show her he meant no harm.

At some point in his walk to her, he'd taken his gun out of its holster. He couldn't remember doing it but was grateful for the smooth wood now steady in his hand. The crowd quieted and stepped back, causing Sterling to turn around.

His eyes narrowed, and his head cocked. "Do we have our first customer?"

Sterling's icy voice filled Robert with righteous anger. The insinuation pushed his breakfast up his throat. He sent a quick prayer heavenward before answering.

"That's about enough of this nonsense." Robert pushed on, though Sterling's jaw clenched in anger at the confrontation. "It's obvious this woman is not a horse thief."

"It's not that obvious to me," someone yelled from the crowd.

"Then you're a fool," Robert boomed. "Her horse is unshod and without a saddle. No white man rides like that."

"She could've left the saddle," another yelled.

"And yanked the horseshoes off?" Robert scoffed. "You think this scrawny, little thing could do that?"

"It doesn't matter." Sterling stepped his horse closer to Robert. "I've staked claim to her. Her past is of little importance to me. Now, are you placing a bid for her first slot or not?"

Robert shook his head and stepped in front of the woman. He was close enough he could feel her breath through his cotton shirt. The warmth of her presence infused him with courage.

"I'll not let you steal this woman into slavery." Robert scanned the crowd of broken men and raised his voice, steeling it with conviction. "Have you men lost all your sense of decency that you would stand in broad daylight and bid on fornication? The war abolished slavery fifteen years ago. What Sterling is doing is slavery, and I, for one, will not stand by and see a human auctioned off like cattle."

"Neither will I," a voice thundered into the fray.

The tension in Robert's muscles eased at the familiar voice of Trapper Dan. Maybe the two of them could push these men along and save this woman's life. He turned his attention back to Sterling and flinched at the recognition that flashed across Sterling's face with a sneer.

"My business is that, mine. Do you two honestly think you can take me on?" Sterling chuckled humorlessly.

The featherlike touch of shaking hands burned Robert's back as soft prayers lifted to his ears. The Spirit of God rushed into him and almost buckled his knees in awe. He stood straighter as purpose coursed through him, and he added his own prayers to hers. He would save her or die trying.

"What is the meaning of this?" A new voice in the conversation made Robert turn to a man who rode up on horseback.

The silver badge pinned to the man's vest glimmered in the sunlight. Robert took a second to glance around, relieved to see most of the men had dispersed. The marshal guided his horse through the crowd, a scowl on his face as he surveyed the scene.

"Nothing but a little fun, Marshal," Sterling offered with his cocky smile.

"I've warned you before, Fitzgerald. Keep your fun within the walls of your tent. Our town may be young, but the government wants to make sure it stays civil." The marshal glared at Sterling. "If I ever hear of you doing business on the streets of my town again, you'll wish you'd never had."

The threat felt empty to Robert, and Sterling's smug smile proved he thought the same. Sterling shrugged and bowed his head toward the marshal in acquiescence.

As Sterling clicked his horse forward, he rode close to Robert. "Don't think I'll forget this, Sweeney." Sterling's voice came out low and menacing, and his fingers flexed where his hand sat upon his leg. "Thought you learned your lesson back home and knew better than to cross me."

"Your intimidation won't work anymore, Sterling." Robert's voice rumbled in his chest.

Sterling huffed a cynical laugh. "We'll see." He eased his horse forward, acting as if he owned the world.

Robert stood where he was until all but Trapper Dan and the marshal cleared out. He turned to the young woman and took a step back. Her dark brown eyes lifted to his, stealing his breath right from his lungs. With her high cheekbones and silky black hair braided in two, she proved more beautiful than Robert had first imagined. The tears that hung in her eyes added to the regal sorrow that lingered on her face.

"Thank you," she whispered up to him.

He nodded his response.

"Sparrow!" Trapper Dan's concerned yell turned them both toward the legendary mountain man.

The young woman covered her mouth as a sob ripped from her. Trapper Dan opened his arms, and she launched herself into them. Trapper Dan bowed his head over her small frame and prayed his thanksgiving to God. Robert added his own, glad the woman had a friend that could take her to safety.

## CHAPTER 3

Sparrow breathed in the smoky wood scent of Dan's leather tunic, letting the familiar smell cleanse her of the filthy stench of the men who had surrounded her. Thank God for the giant stranger who stepped in when no one else had.

"Sparrow, girl, what are you doing here? Dear merciful Lord above, I about ate my stomach backwards. I was so scared when I saw you there." Dan held Sparrow at arm's length, the color returning to his skin. "Land sakes, my heart's bumping like a jackrabbit that just escaped the fox."

Sparrow placed her hand over her chest and agreed with the sentiment. Fear had never choked her like it had in front of that crowd. Death was preferable to the life that Sterling would've forced her into. Sparrow turned to thank the man but found him walking away.

"Robert, hold up," Dan called, causing the man's shoulders to slump as he turned.

Robert approached slowly, his eyes darting around but

never landing on her or Dan. He rubbed his forehead as he walked toward them. Sparrow wondered at his wary spirit when a minute earlier he'd stood as a warrior.

He extended his hand, and with a sigh, met Dan's gaze. "Trapper Dan, nice to see you again."

"And I am so glad to see you, Robert. Thank you for helping Sparrow. I don't know what would've happened if you weren't here to step in." Dan thwacked Robert on the shoulder.

Robert's tanned neck turned red. "I'm glad I could help."

"Thank you." Her words came out a whisper since fear still gripped her voice.

"Sparrow, what in the world are you doing here?" Dan turned his attention back to her. "Are you loco coming here? How could you possibly think it wise to venture into the valley? I—"

Sparrow raised her eyebrow, and Dan's words sputtered to a stop. "I left earlier this summer to visit Orlando and Samara," she said. Robert flinched at the names, but Sparrow continued. "I was gone longer than I wanted. When I saw the area overrun with whites, I was headed to the trail over the mountains to Chief Ouray's band when those sidewinders found me. What happened to my people?"

"As soon as the passes melted, the soldiers came." Robert's low, deep voice rumbled like thunder building in the distance.

"They must have come shortly after I left. I hadn't planned on staying so long." Sparrow caught herself twisting her hands in front of her. She dropped them and pushed her shoulders back. "I need to go now before any more trouble happens. Thank you again for your help."

"Sparrow, it's not safe for you to go anywhere on your own right now." Dan tugged on his beard with a shake of his head.

Sparrow placed her hand on her friend's arm. "Dan, I will be fine once I move out of the valley."

Dan shook his head even harder, and Sparrow prepared for the coming argument. He held a special place in her heart. He'd been a good friend to her and John, always visiting for hours on end when he'd travel by. He had helped her navigate through her sorrow, so she wouldn't hold his next words against him, though she was sure she'd disagree with him.

"Sparrow, I wish it were that simple, but it's not. The mountains are crawling with men like the rabble that were just here. From here practically all the way to Ouray's front door." Dan motioned wide with his hands, almost hitting Robert in the gut.

"You've seen Chief Ouray? Has he been moved as well?" Sparrow hoped the government would at least respect the man who had tried so hard for peace.

"I just came from there. He's fine, if not a little upset at the situation. He'll be traveling south to speak with Chief Ignacio soon." Dan took his wide-brimmed hat off and knocked it against his leg. "That's beside the point, Sparrow. I just ventured through that area, and you can't make it, not on your own."

"I won't travel the trails. I will go through the woods and take the longer, older routes." Sparrow moved to Lightning's side, checking her packs to make sure they were still tight.

Dan stepped up and placed his hands on her shoulders, forcing her to look at him. "You aren't listening. Men are crawling everywhere like a swarm of ants on an anthill. You can't go alone and be safe."

Sparrow rolled her eyes and huffed. Dan had always been a force to reckon with. She knew arguing with him would only delay her departure.

She threw her hands up in defeat. "Fine. Let's get to your horse so we can leave."

Dan's eyes turned sorrowful before he looked away and exhaled. "I can't take you, girl. The Lord is urging me to check in on some old friends. The call is so intense, I can't turn away from it."

Sparrow laughed. "Then why do we bicker? I will pray for you on your journey, my friend."

"Sparrow ..." Dan huffed and glanced at Robert.

Dan's eyes lit and his lips twitched. *Oh, no.* Sparrow's stomach quivered at what the man schemed.

"Robert, I need your help." Dan turned to face Robert. "Sparrow is a very dear friend of mine. I need someone who can offer her the safety of his presence, and I can't think of a more worthy fellow than you. I need you to take her west to Chief Ouray's band."

Robert's eyes bulged briefly before he glanced down and hid behind his hat. He peered out toward the edge of town, then shook his head. Was he inwardly arguing with Dan like she was? Hopefully, he'd finish it and tell Dan he couldn't help, so she could head out on the trail.

Robert turned to Dan, his dark brown eyes shining with determination. "Okay, I'll take her over the mountain."

Sparrow's heart sank. Why would this complete stranger agree to such a thing? "But—"

"Great!" Dan slapped Robert on the shoulder. "I see the marshal still lounging over there. Let's get this ceremony done right quick so you can head out."

Sparrow's head snapped backward at Dan's confusing words. Was there a ceremony the whites did for sending off friends she wasn't aware of? She glanced at Robert to see if he understood the loco mountain man any better. Robert's mouth flapped open and closed repeatedly like a landed trout. He wouldn't be any help.

"Ceremony?" She hated the hesitancy in her voice, like she was peeking in the bushes and wasn't sure what would come out to greet her.

"Well, the wedding, of course," Dan said with exasperation.

"Wedding?" Sparrow and Robert asked in shocked unison.

"You didn't think I'd send you out into the wilderness alone together without marrying, did you?" Dan placed his hands on his hips. "That wouldn't be proper at all."

"Dan—" Sparrow's voice quavered at the sudden onslaught of emotions brought on at the thought of marrying again. How could she, when John and their baby had taken such a large part of her heart with them? And to marry a stranger?

"I know, Sparrow, but Robert is a good man." Robert shook his head while Dan talked. "I trust him to get you safely to your family."

"But marriage? After John, I—"

Dan placed a hand on Sparrow's cheek and stepped close so only she could hear. "The Lord has given you too much love in your heart to bottle it up, Sparrow girl. Trust Him. I feel His leading in this."

"Trapper Dan, could I have a word?" Robert stepped a few feet away with Dan following. Robert dropped his voice, but the low rumble tumbled into Sparrow's ear anyway. "Dan ... I ... how can you trust me with this? Why in the world would you bind your friend to me? You know my past."

"Son, I know your past. I know the things your family did." Dan placed a hand on Robert's shoulder when his head bowed in shame. "I had sensed the Holy Spirit stirring in you, boy. When you turned from your brother's schemes and helped Viola, you took the first step toward redemption. I see the change in your heart, Robert. Heck, I always saw the good inside of you struggling to overcome the evil."

Robert shook his head and sniffed. How was he connected to the Thomas family? He looked back down the road, his shoulders drooping. Something pulled this strong man down, anchoring his spirit low. Sparrow could feel it.

"My farm. I just finished my cabin." The hesitancy in his voice tugged at Sparrow's heart.

"Robert, I tell you what. I'd like to buy your homestead from you. I've been thinking about stopping my wandering ways." Dan pulled at his shaggy beard. "If you two get over the mountain and find you mix like water and oil, and no shenanigans have happened, then you can file an annulment without ever telling anyone you were married to begin with. I'll sell you your homestead back when you return."

Robert glanced at Dan, then turned his gaze on Sparrow. Sorrow etched shadows next to his eyes and lips. His eyebrows drew together, and she wondered if his concern was for her or himself. Dan asked what they thought. With his gaze never leaving hers, Sparrow mirrored Robert's nod of consent.

～

*What in the world have I gotten myself into now?*

Robert wiped the sweat from his hands as inconspicuously as he could. He hadn't planned he'd be getting hitched and trailing off into the mountains when he came into town for beans and bacon. No, he had firmly decided marrying shouldn't be in his future. His family name deserved to end with him. Yet, here he was, listening to Trapper Dan jabber on about the sanctity of marriage while Robert stood next to an Indian goddess. Every time he stole a peek at her, she stole the breath right from his chest.

He wasn't even sure how Trapper Dan had gotten him to agree to this crazy plan. He mentally chided himself. That wasn't true. It was the way Trapper Dan had called Robert son and the forgiveness Robert had seen in his eyes. It was the sense of doing something bigger than Robert's own plans, and the warmth that had spread through him at that thought.

Robert's fields could wait until spring to get plowed. He'd help Sparrow find her people, then come back to his cabin, hopefully before the snow fell. Maybe if he did enough for others, the scales of his good and bad deeds would even out. He knew it'd take whatever he had left of his life to walk the narrow path to the gate of heaven, for those weights to ever tip toward even. He'd reconciled himself to that fact.

Robert now realized it meant more than just keeping his nose down and minding his own business. He could do that until the day he died and not make it to the pearly gates. He'd never make up for his past mistakes that way.

No, in order for him to earn his way, he would have to go out on a limb for God. He'd have to be like Paul the apostle, who Dan liked to talk about so much, going through many trials and hardships to gain forgiveness for his sins. So, Robert would take the beautiful Sparrow across the mountains, follow all the rules laid out before him, and come back to wait for the Lord's next task. Then, he'd live out a life worth living that he so desperately wanted.

"I now pronounce you man and wife," Trapper Dan announced with a flourish. "You may kiss your bride."

Robert jolted at the sudden interruption to his thoughts. Heat raced up his neck and into his cheeks as he gaped at Sparrow. This wasn't part of his plan to stay as distant as possible so his heart didn't stutter with hope. A wife and family couldn't be a permanent part of his future. He couldn't spread his family's curses any further.

Sparrow lifted a sad, understanding smile and turned her cheek up to him. Robert bent and quickly placed a kiss on her soft skin. His heart raced with an unfamiliar feeling, and he rubbed his hand across his chest to ease it.

Trapper Dan chuckled and clapped his hand on Robert's back. "All right. Let's get to your homestead so you can pack up and get on your way."

Robert nodded and headed toward his horse. He thought of all that he didn't have to pack. There really wasn't much at his homestead that he would need. Everything he owned, besides the cabin and meager furniture, could fit in one of his saddlebags.

Robert swung into the saddle and headed out of town. As he passed the last of the tent businesses, a chill slid down his back, and all the hairs on his neck stood on end. He surveyed the hastily pitched tents, searching for the reason for his discomfort.

His gaze slammed to a halt when it collided with Sterling's intense, unyielding stare. He leaned against a sturdy pole connected to an awning. The sign nailed haphazardly to a stick in the dirt read *Sterling's Stellar Starlas.* Sterling slowly lifted his clenched hand, made a gun with his finger and thumb, and shot Robert. Sterling raised an eyebrow as he lowered his hand to his side.

Robert faced forward and pushed his horse into a trot. He stuffed the worry down. Sterling's threat only held weight if Robert allowed it to. He knew it was a lie the minute he thought it, but he hoped the marshal's reprimand and Robert's own size would dissuade Sterling from any further trouble.

Robert led the group back down the same trail he'd just come in on. The birds singing their songs as they flitted through the trees sounded more subdued than when he'd travelled in. The mourning dove's long, soulful call buried itself deep with his spirit.

He scoffed at himself and straightened his back. It wasn't like he'd been sentenced to death or anything. He simply had to adjust his plans a little. So what if he'd have to go through the difficulty of obtaining an annulment? If it kept Sparrow safe and got her to her family, he'd handle the legal headache. So what if he couldn't plow his fields right away? It wasn't like they were going anywhere. He'd just have to work a little harder come spring.

Hard work would be good for him, good for his tortured soul that seemed set on dwelling in his past. How would he make it through the long winter without a project to keep his mind from lingering where he didn't want it to? Robert shook off the troubling thought. He needed to focus on the job God planted before him, not the worry of tomorrow.

Robert pulled to a stop at his place and dismounted. Without looking around, for fear he'd change his mind, he stomped into the cabin and grabbed his Bible, the rest of Linc's coins, and a few other items. He took one last look around and marched out the door.

Sparrow stood in his yard, gazing past the trees and creek to Mount Sopris. "Robert, you picked your land well." Sparrow peered up at him and pointed toward the creek. "I used to come here to be alone. I sat on that boulder, watched birds flit around, and prayed. We both picked this spot as a special place. That is no surprise to God."

Robert's chest constricted as she touched her heart, a small smile on her face. She'd just been married off to a man whose past was shadier than a cave at midnight, and here she stood, finding a connection the two of them held. He swallowed hard and looked over the land he'd taken weeks to locate.

"That would explain the peace I felt when I found this place," Robert mumbled. When Sparrow's eyebrows scrunched together, he added, "Well, your prayers soaked into the earth until the very rocks cried out." He rubbed the back of his neck, not sure why he didn't keep his big trap shut. "I stopped just to get a drink, but when I leaned up against that boulder and felt the warmth of God within my heart, I knew I'd finally found where God wanted me."

Sparrow's smile stretched across her face, and joy filled her eyes. She gazed around again and took a deep breath in. He would have to make sure he kept his eyes on the trail and not gawking at the woman he was tasked with protecting.

"This here is a mighty fine homestead you've got." Trapper Dan extended his hand with a pouch in it. "Here's money for the land and cabin. If you decide to come back, just give me the pouch back, and we'll call it good."

Robert took the pouch and peeked in. His eyes widened at the amount of coins inside. He quickly extended it back to Trapper Dan and opened his mouth.

"Now, Robert, don't be contrary." Trapper Dan crossed his arms, effectively cutting off Robert's ability to give the money back. "This is prime land that will just gain more value as people flock in. You've built a beautiful, sturdy cabin that I don't have to take the time to build. If you come back, you can give the pouch back to me. If not, well, it's money well spent. Come you two, let's pray so you can get on the trail."

Trapper Dan grabbed Robert's and Sparrow's hands and waited until they held each other's hand. As they stood in the circle, Trapper Dan prayed for protection and a willingness to follow God's plan. The heat of the Holy Spirit started in his gut and spread through his body. As Trapper Dan pulled Sparrow into a fatherly hug, Robert added his own silent, fervent prayer that God would guide his feet to the right path and keep the hellhounds of his past off of their trail.

# CHAPTER 4

ROBERT STRETCHED his long legs toward the campfire and marveled at the meal Sparrow had roasting over the fire. She had shot the rabbit with her bow before he'd even seen the critter. In fact, he'd learned so much from her in the last two days since they'd been on the trail, he wondered how he and his brothers had even survived one winter in the mountains. The little huntress kept surprising him with facts and findings that had him seeing the Colorado mountains in a whole new way.

To make matters worse, Sparrow had a patience and kindness to her that surpassed anyone he'd ever met, except maybe his dear ma. She hadn't laughed at him when he made a mess butchering one of the grouse she had shot the day before. She'd simply kneeled beside him with the second bird and asked if she could show him how her people did it. No ridicule or condescension, just a kind offer of a different way.

She'd shown him how to make a small, smokeless fire so they didn't draw attention to themselves and the different roots and berries they could collect for their meals, since they'd left in such haste there had been little to pack but a bag of jerky he'd made. All the skills would come in handy once he was back on his own, and she'd shared it all with a tender heart.

Which only furthered Robert down the path to the conundrum he found himself in. He was falling headfirst into the dangerous abyss of love with a wife he wasn't intending to keep. He supposed it wasn't actually love; maybe it was just respect. Whatever it was, it had a mighty strong pull on him.

If it was just her beauty drawing him in, he could easily stifle that feeling. Hadn't he been doing that for years, since he realized he never wanted to subject a woman to his family? But adding her ingenuity and gentle spirit to the mix was too much to combat. She didn't shy away from his big frame while he lumbered around camp at night, but plopped down right next to him to enjoy the scenery. She didn't jest when he mumbled about not learning how to do something as simple as gutting a bird but asked where he had been raised if it wasn't in the mountains.

He hadn't lied when he'd told her he'd grown up in St. Louis, but when she'd asked about his childhood, he told her more of the marvels of the city than the depravity of his upbringing. He didn't need to burden her with his filth, and she seemed to catch the hint and acted interested in his descriptions of the river, levee, and the steamboats that made their way up and down the river.

Mostly he tried to keep his mouth shut and his thoughts to himself. Maybe if he didn't interact with her too much, he could escape back to his cabin without his heart being ripped from his body. Robert rubbed his chest at the thought, then scoffed at himself. He was being mighty theatrical over someone who hadn't shown the slightest interest in him past friendship.

A twig snapped in the woods off to Robert's right. He tensed, turning his head that way and sliding his Colt from its holster. Leaves rustled under a footstep. Robert cocked his gun slowly to make as little noise as possible.

"Robert?" Sparrow's soft, melodic voice floated in the air.

Robert heaved a sigh of relief and uncocked his gun. His muscles ached with the tension running through him. He closed his eyes and took another deep breath, forcing his muscles to relax. He opened his eyes to see Sparrow emerging from the forest like those mythical wood nymphs his ma always read stories about, a soft smile tilting her lips up and amusement twinkling in her eyes.

*Oh, Lord. How am I supposed to not love her? Help me be strong and follow a path honorable to her.*

He wasn't sure if it was the devil tempting him or the Lord testing him, but he doubted he could stay detached on his strength alone.

*What therefore God hath joined together, let not man put asunder.*

The verse slammed into his mind in Trapper Dan's booming voice. Robert almost glanced around to see where the wily mountain man was. That verse finding his brain just proved how desperate and weak he really was. He'd have to double down on his prayers and diligence.

"Robert, I'm impressed." She stepped noiselessly into camp, carrying two grouse.

He quickly got to his feet and approached, taking the

birds from her hands. "How's that?" It surprised him that his voice worked around the brick lodged in his throat.

"I made just a small noise, and yet you heard." Sparrow gazed up at him with those beautiful almond-shaped eyes, sparkling joy replacing the solemness that often lingered there.

What exactly caused her expression to appear miles away? It wasn't sadness, per se, but something akin. The fact that he'd been able to displace it with happiness made him a little lightheaded. His neck heated when he realized he still hadn't responded to her statement, but stood like a giant statue, staring.

He turned his attention to the grouse and shrugged. "Guess you're rubbing off on me."

Her laughter tinkled like a thousand bells and slammed into his gut with such force that it busted it to pieces, leaving fluttering butterflies where solid organs should be. This was what happened when he let his mind wander onto unacceptable trails. If he didn't get a hold of his thoughts, when this task finished, he'd be left brainless, with no way to navigate home and the memories of her laughter haunting his dreams.

∽

SPARROW WATCHED in awe as Robert shuttered his feelings right in front of her. He stuffed all his emotions into a drawstring bag, then cinched it closed so tightly she doubted a flea could get in. With a stoic nod, he took the grouse to the little mountain stream they camped next to and deftly got them ready for the fire—just like she'd taught him.

Something haunted this surprise husband of hers. Some demons of his past circled like vultures above him, diving occasionally to pick at exposed flesh. She'd dreamed it last night, saw Robert's anguish as he tried to fend them off. She'd woken with a start and stared at her husband over the embers that cast a soft glow on his face. Even in sleep, he remained guarded, his body stiff and his handsome face pinched.

She checked the rabbit roasting over the fire and watched Robert as he meticulously cleaned the grouse breasts of every feather and undesirable bit. He was intelligent, this city man. Watching and absorbing everything she said as if he needed to get it right and perfect.

His discomfort with her showed in his every action. She'd noticed right quick that he attempted to make himself seem smaller, like he worried his size intimidated her. She'd never seen another man as big as Robert, with him rivaling a grizzly bear in size, but it didn't scare her or make her uncomfortable. His lean, strong muscles and tall stature comforted her in a way she hadn't expected. She enjoyed sitting next to him and feeling his heat radiate toward her as they surveyed the woods around their campsite or when they stopped for a quick lunch.

What amazed her most about this man was his care of her. Not that he gushed affection like she'd seen so many bucks do. No, it was the way he slowly picked at his food until she sat back and sighed with contentment. Only then did he eat the meager serving he took for himself and anything left of the meal. It was how he'd given her a plate of meat, commenting how that little bit was his favorite. His favorite, and yet he'd given it to her.

His concern didn't stop there. The night before, he'd

found the most level ground, cleared it of every stick and rock possible, then had laid out her bedroll. She glanced around the camp and smiled at her blanket set upon a pile of fallen leaves in the most protected spot in the camp. She also didn't miss the fact that Robert's bedroll wasn't upon a fluffy bed but exposed and placed where he could lie as sentry through the night.

No one had ever taken such care of her, not even John. Sparrow closed her eyes to the shame that thought brought. John had been a great, loving husband. She would've never thought such a thing without the contrast Robert presented.

She shouldn't compare the two. Where John was refined with a confidence in the love of God, she sensed Robert's life had been shadowed in darkness. Where John had grown up in the comfort of wealth, she guessed Robert had only known poverty.

Robert's soft footsteps made their way back to the fire. How the big man walked almost silently amazed Sparrow. While he was city-bred, he was born to be a mountain man. She opened her eyes as a small smile tweaked her lips. His forehead scrunched in concern as he searched the area. His gaze connected with hers, and he faltered with the grouse meat.

"I, um, I'm not sure what to do with this." Robert lifted the meat up in a shrug.

She stepped to him with a smile. "I will smoke it. We will have meat for breakfast. Have you ever smoked meat before?"

He rubbed his hand through his thick, dark brown hair, making it stick out in all directions. "I've smoked venison before."

Sparrow nodded, remembering the jerky so tough and dry she almost hadn't been able to swallow it. If they weren't traveling so fast, she'd teach him how to smoke meat properly. As it was, she determined to teach him everything she could.

"Do you want to see how to smoke these?" She held her breath, wondering why her heart raced for his answer.

He nodded without looking at her. Her heart shrank slightly, and she pressed her lips together. She didn't want her heart affected at all. She wasn't willing to risk it again. Taking a deep breath and asking the Lord to focus her mind on what was important, she pushed her feelings aside and went about showing Robert how to smoke grouse.

"Do you see those green branches?" She pointed to the pile she'd gathered earlier, and he nodded. "Bring those over. We'll weave them to make a stand over the pit."

Sparrow set the grouse on a clean rock and showed him how to weave the branches into a loose basket. They worked on opposite sides of the branches, their knees touching. When his stiff fingers snapped a branch, he huffed in disgust and glared at his hands. She reached across the branches and slid her fingers up his.

He stilled like a frightened deer in the woods. Grabbing one large hand that was almost twice the size of hers, she examined it, holding it in both of hers as she turned it over. She ran her fingers over scars and calluses, trying to ignore the way his hand trembled and her heart raced.

"These long fingers God has given you are good for the wilderness. They are strong and lean, not short and fat like sausages." Sparrow chuckled, peeking up at Robert.

He glared at his hands, his lip lifting in a sneer. She tilted her head as her eyes grew warm. How could this amazing man have such hate for himself? What was it that bound him tight to his doubts, not allowing God's love to penetrate the darkness and dispel his demons? He spent any spare time they had reading the Bible he'd packed, but she wondered if he truly understood it. She wanted to help him see his worth and truly trust in God.

Sparrow lifted his hand and softly kissed his palm. Robert inhaled sharply and tried to pull away. She held on and pressed his palm to her cheek.

"You are a good man, Robert." When he shook his head in contradiction, she squeezed his fingers and moved his hand so his palm pressed against her collarbone. "I feel it here, that whisper from God I won't argue with."

Robert stared at her, his eyes wide and shining. His breath hitched in his chest, and she wished to pull him into her arms and just hold him. Instead, she pulled his hand up and kissed his palm again before placing it on the weaved branches.

"Relax, Robert. Relax your spirit, your heart, and your hands. Life, like these branches, does not have to be forced into place." She nodded toward the weave. "Finish this while I work on dinner, and then I will show you what to do next."

He nodded absentmindedly, his fingers flexing on the branches. She stood and pulled the rabbit off the fire, keeping Robert in her vision. He inhaled and rolled his shoulders as he let the breath out. Slowly, he wove the branches, occasionally shaking his hands as if to loosen them.

Sparrow's heart broke at his hesitancy. The day they'd

left, after her emotions settled from her incident in town and they were well on their way, she'd inwardly questioned the need for the rushed marriage. She knew full well that had Dan been able to go, she wouldn't be married to *him*, though the situation was the same. She hadn't wanted to marry ever again. Now, however, as she finished dinner, trying hard not to watch her new husband, she knew God had arranged for her and Robert to marry. Not for her protection, but for his freedom. She would lean on God's will, knowing she might never understand His reasoning, and help her gentle giant find his place in God.

# CHAPTER 5

⁂

ROBERT TRIED to scan the area as they travelled along the Ute trail, but his gaze always returned to Sparrow in front of him. He flexed his fingers and rubbed the palm that still burned from her touch. Her words echoed in his head, taunting him.

He couldn't relax when it came to her … couldn't relax, period.

The minute he did, the plagues of his past, his own weaknesses, would overcome him. Didn't God say in Exodus chapter fifteen to do what is right in the sight of God, listen to His commandments, and keep all His laws? God promised if Robert did all of that, He'd heal Robert. He desperately needed that healing for his putrid heart, black with generations of sin.

Robert had written that verse in the front of his Bible. He read it every time he opened the Word. He knew there were many laws of God. He'd started at the beginning of the Bible and was working his way through. He'd seen what would happen if he didn't follow them diligently.

Weren't the Israelites always turning from God's way and suffering for it? Robert had made it all the way through Ecclesiastes, and though a lot of it made little sense to him, he had understood the depth of his need to never turn away from the law of God.

Then, along came Sparrow, his temporary wife, spouting nonsense at him to relax. That life couldn't be forced. He shook his head as he scanned the trees. He didn't want to force anything. He had enough force in his life to last an eternity. No, forcing life had nothing to do with it. He simply needed to control himself, his actions, his thoughts, his words. Accomplishing that task kept getting harder and harder to do the longer he spent with Sparrow.

God knew Robert shouldn't have a wife and family. His own mother had whispered words of the Sweeney curse on her deathbed, urging him to put an end to it. God truly was trying Robert, testing his conviction to keep his distance from Sparrow. Not only did she seem at ease in his presence, but her touch yesterday had ripped something hard off his heart. He felt the foundation of his resolve weakening.

Then, to add insult to his dilemma, Robert moved from Ecclesiastes to Song of Solomon last night. *Let him kiss me with the kisses of his mouth.* The second verse slammed into his consciousness again as his eyes moved back to Sparrow on her horse. Never had he so easily memorized a verse as that one, repeating it without thought over and over again as he had stared across the low fire, watching her sleep.

Why would he come to that book now? Why couldn't he be reading the testing of Job with boils and sackcloth instead of the pursuit of a beguiling bride? Maybe Robert should just skip Song of Solomon for now, come back to it when he had a better handle on life, far away from the temptation of Sparrow's generous lips and sparkling eyes.

*No*, he thought with a shake of his head. That would be taking the easy route. He'd set out on this course to learn God's Word. He wouldn't shirk it just because it made his heart race with anxious longing and his walls weaken like Jericho's.

Sparrow disappeared around a bend in the trail up ahead. A cold hand squeezed Robert's heart, and his palms slicked where he gripped the reins. He eased his horse into a trot to close the gap between them. Coming around the turn, his eyes narrowed at the sight before him.

Three men blocked the trail in front of Sparrow. Their filthy clothes hung on their bodies like so many men he'd seen over the years. Prospectors. Not very good ones at that, from the look of the ramshackle camp off the trail. They leered up at Sparrow with hate and an eagerness that made Robert's blood run cold.

"Well, look what we got here, and just when I was getting plumb bored. Now we's got ourself some entertainment." The man closest to her wiped his hand across his mouth and stepped closer.

Sparrow sat on her horse, her back straight and her head held high. Just like before, Robert's little warrior showed no fear. Everything in him wanted to dig for his cannon and let bullets fly, but he also knew that wouldn't please God. He took a deep breath and prayed for wisdom and to keep his head.

"Boys." He inwardly smiled when the one word caused the men to jump.

Were they so focused on their lustful thoughts that they hadn't noticed him approach? Sparrow turned her head and gazed at him as he came even with her. A calm and confident expression shone from her face as her eyes connected with his. She gave him a small nod before turning back to the men. How could she have such belief in him?

Robert turned his attention back to the men, determined to prove her trust was well placed. "The pickings must be slow if you boys are greeting travelers. You with one of those companies from Leadville, or are you prospecting for yourself?"

The men looked to each other before the bigger one standing up front spoke. "We're our own men." He tapped his shirt in pride, causing a puff of dust to float into the air.

"Well, I hope you have success. I know these mountains are ripe for the picking." Robert eased his horse forward to pass.

The man in front squinted at Robert, then his finger shook up and down as a sly smile crossed his face. "I know you. You're Robert Sweeney." The man's jovial expression faded as he glanced around the woods nervously, causing Robert's gut to sour. "Where are those brothers of yours?"

"Dead."

The word caused a second of stillness before the men's shoulders relaxed.

"That's a right shame," the man said. "But I see you've done for yourself all right. Now, speaking of ripe for the pickings, you're one right smart fella, bringing a painted cat out to the lonely men on the hunt."

Robert glared at the man with all the fury he buried deep. "This is my wife." His words ground out low and deadly, causing the man's eyes to widen. "Apologize for your disrespect."

The man's Adam's apple bobbed as he took a step back. "Sorry there, Sweeney, I didn't real—"

"To her, not to me." Robert motioned to Sparrow.

"So-sorry, Mrs. Sweeney, for our disrespect," the man stammered as he whipped his hat off his head and took another step back.

"I forgive you and pray you seek forgiveness from God as well." She smiled sweetly at the men.

"Sparrow, honey, why don't you head on up the trail. I won't be but a second behind." Robert motioned toward the direction they'd been traveling.

She nodded at him, then smiled at the men. How she could look at them with a peaceful smile amazed Robert. His eyes followed her until she was several paces ahead. He inhaled, wanting to exude the forgiveness his wife had shown.

"I'll be praying that you men find success here." Robert motioned to the camp and woods surrounding them before focusing back on the men. "I'll also be praying that you take a good hard look at your lives and turn them over to God. I plan on living out eternity in streets of gold, not constant anguish like my brothers. Though devilish ways may tempt us in our short life here on earth, being Lucifer's riding partner through the depths of hell is not something I wish to sign on to anymore."

The men scuffed their worn-out boots in the dirt and mumbled that they'd think on it as they turned back to their camp. Pity and relief warred within Robert. A deep sorrow welled up for the mountain full of men willing to chase the devil down the trail of life. Maybe he should think about traveling the mountains, sharing the Good News like Trapper Dan. He bowed his head as he urged his horse forward, thanking God for leading him to the path of life.

∼

Sparrow peeked at Robert over her mug as she took a drink. She wasn't sure what to do with the information about Robert's family she'd learned from the men. How had she not known her life was connected to a Sweeney, the family who had terrorized her friends and murdered a man she'd respected deeply? How had Dan ever thought it would be okay to bind her forever to that horrid family?

She closed her eyes and inhaled the cleansing smell of the bubbling creek they'd set their camp up next to and the comforting smoke from the fire. The rush of water tumbling over the rocks and the birds chattering back and forth only magnified her turmoil. She pulled the blanket around her shoulders tighter as a cold autumn wind snuck through camp. She'd questioned God repeatedly after the run in with the miners. God kept leading her back to the fact that Dan had said he trusted Robert. The man before her was not a man who would kidnap women and kill men. Yet, she couldn't ignore the fear that had caused the men's muscles to tighten and their eyes to dart like cornered rabbits. Hadn't she sensed a darkness in Robert from their first night on the trail?

She opened her eyes and found him staring at her. He quickly lowered his eyes to the Bible open on his outstretched legs before him. He hadn't said more than a handful of words to her since they'd had the run in with the men.

Though her mind screamed at her to let her questions be, her heart couldn't obey. "Did you take part in killing Joseph Thomas?"

The question settled in the air like a wet blanket, stifling and heavy. His chin dropped to his chest, and his shoulders shuddered on his deep breath. He slowly closed the Bible and rubbed his hands on the cover.

"Yeah." His voice cracked, and he cleared his throat. "Joseph's death pulls tight around my neck like a noose." He adjusted his collar and rolled his shoulders.

"What happened?" She forced the words out.

"Linc, my brother, wanted something Joseph had. Linc always wanted what others had." Robert sighed and rubbed his hand through his hair. "He got tired of sneaking around, trying to figure out where Joseph's gold mine was, so we jumped Joseph to get him to talk. I hated what we were doing, could hardly keep my stomach from escaping my throat. Joseph had always been friendly enough to us, even though he had to know we were hanging around and up to no good. I even caught him leaving a deer rump next to our shack one winter."

Robert looked away and sniffed. He picked up a stick and tossed it into the fire. Anguish radiated from him. Sparrow pulled her knees up to her chest and wrapped her arms around her legs. She wanted to rush his story along, but felt the Holy Spirit urging her to hold her tongue.

"I got sick of Linc crowing that he'd bested the great

Joseph Thomas, so I took William and went hunting. I planned to let Joseph go as soon as Linc fell asleep, but …"

A tear trailed down Robert's cheek and caught in his beard. He sniffed and closed his eyes, another tear escaping. The droplets startled her. She'd rarely seen a man cry before.

"But Linc had killed Joseph while we were gone, forced us to leave him there for the animals."

"No." She gasped.

"The guilt of what we did … I couldn't sleep. Was sick to my stomach all the time. Then we stumbled upon Trapper Dan. It'd been a rough week since things hadn't gone Linc's way with Viola, and Linc hated Dan. Normally, I didn't listen much, because why would God care about a Sweeney. But that night, I couldn't not listen." Robert ran his hand through his hair again. "I can't even remember what Trapper Dan said, but the next morning when we left, I knew I couldn't be a part of what Linc did. I'd go scouting with Linc, trying to get him to consider a different path or stay at camp, keeping William with me when I could."

"Why didn't you just leave?"

Robert pushed to his feet and stalked to the other side of camp. He rubbed his arm across his eyes before turning. Her heart clenched at his reddened eyes and stooped posture.

"Because family sticks together, always." The words sounded bitter, and his mouth twisted.

"I don't understand."

"It's the Sweeney way, beaten into us as a babe. Family always sticks together."

"But why, especially when they do such evil?"

"I guess you wouldn't understand, would you? Christians never do." Hurt tinted his sarcastic tone. "Maybe my heart drips just as black as theirs? But you wouldn't understand that either."

Robert turned and stomped into the woods. Sparrow's stomach knotted as she laid her forehead on her knees. Why had she pushed? Why had she allowed her heart to rush her mouth with words when her brain knew better? A sob broke from her chest.

It didn't matter what Robert had done before, not really. If God could cast sins as far as the east is from the west, shouldn't she also? She knew the man Robert was now. He was kind and generous, always thinking of her first before himself. She'd heard the words he'd told the miners as she'd rode away. His low voice had carried on the wind and wound around her heart. After making sure she was safe, he'd been willing to share the hope of God with men who'd thought such vile thoughts toward her. A man whose heart dripped black wouldn't do that.

*Family sticks together, huh?* Sparrow lifted her head from her knees with that thought. A small smile tweaked her lips as she wiped her tears away. She supposed that family virtue held merit, especially now that she was Robert's family.

She tinkered around camp, cleaning up supper and repacking their things for the morning. Darkness settled, and stars blinked in the sky. Robert still hadn't returned when the moon was high and the flames of the fire burned low, though she could sense him patrolling the shadows around the camp. She wrapped herself tight against the frigid wind that signaled winter's approach into the bedroll Robert had fashioned for her. She closed her eyes and prayed for his safety, for his tender heart, and for her to be brave. She didn't know what to say or do when he returned, so she prayed God would guide her.

Robert's almost-silent footsteps dragged through the leaves, the sound laying solemnly on her shoulders. She peeked through slitted eyes as he added a few logs to the fire and settled into his bed. Her eyes burned at his slumped shoulders and haggard face. He didn't look her way once, just pulled the scant blanket over his body and rolled away from the fire.

Sparrow sat up. An intense focus on her husband pushed the regret aside. Sin no longer stained his heart, and she meant to show him that. She silently gathered her bedroll and tiptoed around the fire.

Robert pushed to his elbow when she plopped her bundle down next to him. "Sparrow? Wha—"

"I'm cold." She straightened her blankets close to Robert and got between them.

He pushed up to his hand. "I'll get more wood."

Sparrow grabbed his arm, and a fluttery feeling sprang from her chest. "The fire's fine, as long as I have you close."

Robert's eyes opened so wide she thought they might pop out. Stifling a giggle, she laid down not a handbreadth away from him. He swallowed so hard she heard it, and he lay rigid on his side, next to her.

She waited several seconds for him to relax. When he didn't, she glanced up at his face. It was shadowed with the campfire behind him, but she could tell he stared into the woods behind her.

"Robert?" He turned his gaze to her, and, though she

couldn't actually see it, goosebumps raised upon her skin. "I'm glad family sticks together."

"Why?" Doubt filled his whispered question.

"Because, I'm your family now." Sparrow closed the inches that separated them, sighing as she placed her hand on his chest.

He didn't pull her close or touch her, and that was all right with her. She could wait as long as it took for him to realize what she said was genuine. Until then, she'd just have to pray for her words and actions to show truth. She closed her eyes with a contented sigh and fell quickly asleep.

## CHAPTER 6

SPARROW NEVER IMAGINED she was the impatient type. When she'd woken with Robert still sleeping stiffly beside her, his arms glued to his side, she'd silently huffed that the strong lengths hadn't found their way around her during the night. She had smiled sweetly at him as she'd pushed away and sat up while he had stared at her like she was a rattler waiting to strike. She'd said good morning and had gotten busy making them a quick breakfast.

She also never imagined she'd long for another man's arms around her after John. Yet here she rode, wondering what it would feel like to be wrapped in Robert's strong embrace. Her heart lifted at how God knew her intimate desires better than she did.

Robert had packed up their things and taken care of the horses. She had watched him steal glances her way, his brows pulling in and his hands restless as they checked and rechecked their packs. He had thanked her softly for breakfast, then went back to his pacing and fretting.

Sparrow turned in her saddle to peer at Robert and

caught him staring at her. He nodded as his neck pinked, then turned his attention out over the side of the mountain.

She stifled her chuckle before raising her voice. "Robert, it's a tight trail up ahead, and rocky. Keep a sharp eye. No tumbling down the mountain. You keep me too warm at night to lose you now."

His head snapped forward, and his eyes bulged. She smiled widely at him and turned her attention forward. Convincing her husband to relax and enjoy God's forgiveness would be fun.

Sparrow held the reins loosely as Lightning plodded along the narrow trail. She sighed as the wind buffeted her face when the trees gave way to a rocky mountainside. This stretch of the trail always set her heart to racing. Whether from fear or exhilaration, she hadn't decided yet. She forced herself to look over the steep cliff that dropped sharply from the trail. The wind rushed past her again, pulling her hair to whip behind her. The verse about flying on wings of eagles floated on the wind, and she tipped her head back, lifting her arms to the side.

"Sparrow, are you loco?" Robert's tense voice flew up to her.

With her eyes closed and the Spirit of God lifting her thoughts, she hollered back to him. "Haven't you read the verse about mounting up with wings as eagles?"

"I … I guess I haven't gotten to that part."

She dropped her hands and glanced back at him where he looked nervously over the edge. "What do you mean?"

"Exactly what I said. I just finished Song of Solomon last night and started Isaiah this morning. Unless I've forgotten the verse, I haven't gotten to it yet." He rolled his shoulders, his trepidation evident in his sharp tone.

"You're reading the Bible from the start?" A deeper understanding of her husband built in her head.

"Well, it is a book, isn't it? That's how they are supposed to be read." His snippy tone amused her. "How else am I supposed to know how to be a Christian?"

The words rumbled and shook in her head, telling her more about his motives than the last three days with him had. She paused in her speculation, her head whipping toward a place above them on the mountain. Her breath caught in her chest.

"Rockslide!" Sparrow yelled as she kicked Lightning forward.

As if sensing the danger, the horse took off. Sparrow closed her mouth as a cloud of debris cloaked around her like thick fog. Dust filled her nose, choking her. The sound of the mountain grumbling as it sloughed off its side grew like an oncoming freight train. Pelting pebbles turned to stones that turned to small boulders as she and Lightning raced on the skinny trail toward the trees. A stone hit her hard in the head, knocking her off balance.

"Sparrow!" The anguish in Robert's voice had her gripping her knees and pulling herself tight to Lightning's back, winding her fingers into Lightning's mane to anchor herself.

The trail widened, and the safety of the trees beckoned her. She entered the forest and pulled to a stop. Her heart pumped so hard in her chest she thought it would pound right out and gallop away. She slid off Lightning's back as Robert stopped next to her. Dust covered him from head to toe, and he'd never looked more handsome. Her feet hit the ground, but her knees buckled from under her.

Robert caught her before she crumpled into the dirt and pulled her to his chest. His breath sounded ragged, and his heart thundered against her ear. He pulled her closer. One arm wrapped tightly around her waist while the other hand slid up her spine to cradle her head. He pulled his hand away and stared at it, his face blanching white under the grime. She turned her gaze to his hand, and her knees threatened to buckle again from the sight of blood that dripped from his palm.

"You're hurt." Robert wiped his hand on his pants and swooped her into his arms as if she were a child.

His gaze darted frantically around, his breathing increasing even more. Sparrow pointed to a downed aspen just off the trail. He hurried to it and gently set her down like she was a delicate flower. He turned and raced back to the horses, quickly tying them to branches and digging into his pack. She chuckled at his urgency, then stopped when the action made her head hurt more.

Sliding to the ground, she rested her back against the tree. Gingerly, she probed her scalp. Her fingertips slicked with wet warmth. Breakfast turned in her stomach, and she winced at the sharp pain the probing caused.

"Stop. Your hands are filthy." He scowled as he stomped back over with a small bag and the canteens.

He kneeled and reached for her hands. He took them in his and poured water over them. He then dug out his handkerchief from his pocket and wiped the blood and filth from her hands with slow, soothing strokes. His hands shook as he finished and took a deep breath. She leaned forward and buried her face into his neck and wrapped her arms around him.

"I thought … you almost …" Robert's breath shuddered out, his embrace tightening around her.

She pushed back and placed her hand on his dust-coated cheek. "Robert, I'm all right."

His gaze slowly roamed every inch of her face. He pushed her hair behind her ear, his fingers skimming along her jawline. His scrutiny stopped on her lips. Warmth flooded her belly and rushed to her limbs. Robert leaned forward with excruciating slowness.

Would his kiss be as gentle as his hands, or would it hold the bridled yearning she felt within herself? He abandoned his approach with a shake of his head and plopped back with a puff of dust. He stared at his palms and shook his head again before rummaging through the bag.

Sparrow huffed in frustration as he pulled out a roll of bandages and quickly washed his hands with water from the canteen. If her husband wouldn't kiss her after escaping a life-and-death situation, she wondered if he'd ever kiss her. Then again, the desire she saw burning in his eyes gave her hope that he wasn't as unaffected by her as he let on. She smiled when he finally looked over at her. He squinted, his mouth pressing tightly into a line.

"I'm going to take a look at your head." Robert lined up bandages on the tree.

He moved behind her and gently separated her hair. She gritted her teeth against the pain and gazed up at the mountain trail they'd just survived. Something about the rockslide sat wrong with her.

"Robert, when you're done fussing, I will go look." She pointed to the top of the rocky slope.

"Fussing? You're bleeding like a stuck pig, woman."

Sparrow smiled at his miffed tone. She reached back to touch the wound, only to have him swat her hand away.

She chuckled. "If it needs stitches, do it. Otherwise, I'm going."

"Why are you so all-fired anxious to get up there? Haven't we had enough excitement for the day?" Robert's tone was hard, but his ministrations were soft.

Sparrow didn't take offense, figuring he was still as shook up as she was. "My people have traveled this trail for generations. Slides happen in other places but never here. Why?"

"Rockslides happen all the time in the mountains, Sparrow. Why waste our time?"

"Only a fool wouldn't know his enemy, and I didn't marry a fool."

He sighed deeply, the exhale blowing her hair and sending tingles down her spine. "I wouldn't be so sure about that."

His soft words rattled her heart and galvanized her determination. She would prove to her cranky husband just what kind of man he really was. But first, she had a sidewinder to see to.

∼

ROBERT SULKED behind Sparrow as she marched up the mountain. He had barely gotten her head cleaned when she took off for the steep slope, only faltering when she had first stood up. He'd hidden the horses in the woods, then sprinted up the cliff to catch up to her.

How was he to keep her safe and get her to her family when she insisted on chasing troubles? They'd barely made it out of the tumbling rocks the first time. Now she wanted to race to the top of the mountain to look for some imagined foe.

He rolled his shoulders at the pain radiating from where rocks had pelted him. The ache reminded him of when his father had beaten him as a child, and the onslaught had likely bruised his back black and blue. He was just thankful only the one rock had hit Sparrow, though the thought of that made him lightheaded all over again. Those few seconds when she'd teetered on the edge of her horse's back had been the scariest of his life. Yet, if she kept forging ahead like she was, he worried his moments of terror were just beginning.

He snorted a self-deprecating laugh. Who was he kidding? He'd been fearful from the moment he'd said "I do." Fearful that his taint would rub on to her. So, he'd kept his distance and did what needed done. Then, those men had to go and ruin everything.

Robert knew he couldn't hide from his past forever. The possibility of someone recognizing him had been a risk he'd been willing to take to stay in the mountains he loved. He just always figured he'd be the only one to suffer the consequences of his grisly past.

His dread had built as they had continued up the trail the day before, knowing that he couldn't ignore who he really was anymore. The men's reaction to his family hammered the nail into the coffin of any chance Sparrow might respect him. Not that it really mattered, what with him determined to head back to his cabin when this trek was done, giving her the freedom she deserved.

He'd seen the tightness in her face and the hesitation as they'd settled into camp. The words the men had said had chased away their comfort with each other, replacing it with a sense of doom as they'd tiptoed around each other.

He had hoped, even prayed, to his shame, that she would drop the topic of his family. He had dragged his feet all night, a sour taste in his mouth, wondering what she'd ask. He'd almost vomited the small amount of dinner he had forced down when she had asked about Joseph. She certainly knew how to spear right to the heart of an issue. He hadn't meant to snap at her, hadn't wanted to prove again his heritage with his anger. But his hurt had surfaced as anger as he'd stomped off in a huff.

However, he didn't know what she'd been playing at, moving her bedroll to his side of the fire when he'd finally slinked back to camp. Not only that, but she'd lain so near, her faint, fresh scent had enveloped him and dissolved the rest of his foundation.

*I'm your family now.* Sparrow's words echoed through his brain.

There was no way she actually meant that. If he wasn't careful and restrained, his whole resolve would crumble at her feet. It had taken every ounce of willpower not to drape his arm around her and pull her close.

"Robert, quick, come look." Sparrow pointed to the ground before her.

He growled as he pulled himself the rest of the way up the last edge. Not everyone could scamper up a cliff like a mountain goat. Plus, he had the extra job of being ready to catch her if she got lightheaded and fell. He still wasn't convinced her wound didn't need more attention.

He stalked over to her, making sure to glare a bit on his approach. She glanced over at him and flashed her stunning smile. He was glad he'd been glaring, otherwise it would've blinded him.

He stopped next to her and placed his hands on his hips. "Well?"

"Look at these gouges." She crouched and pointed to the dirt before her.

Sure enough, even he couldn't miss the deep scratches that marred the dirt. He bent to study them more closely. He crawled forward, following them to where they stopped, and peeked over the edge of the mountain. His stomach dropped, and a shiver ghosted up his spine at the mass of rocks that now completely blocked the trail.

Robert scooted back from the ledge and turned to Sparrow, who searched the flat outcropping, her head swinging back and forth. He stood and scanned the area. Depressions that could be footprints dotted the ground. Directly behind the gouges were deeper prints that appeared as if a foot had slipped.

"Robert!" Sparrow scurried over a pile of rocks, disappearing from his sight.

Robert rushed to the boulders and climbed up them. She stood on the opposite side, holding long skinny trees. She turned them this way and that, examining them.

"See the ends here?" Sparrow held them up.

He nodded. "They must've been used as leverage to push the boulders over the edge. Once those started rolling, everything below it tumbled down upon us."

The hairs on the back of his neck stood on end. "Someone tried to kill us."

Sparrow glanced up at him, her eyes burning with fury. "The polecats are too afraid to fight like warriors. Ugh, I'm mad enough to swallow a horn toad backwards."

Robert rubbed his hand across his mouth to hide his smile.

She threw down the trees with force. "Backstabbing cowards."

Her words sobered his amusement. Hadn't he been exactly that after leaving St. Louis? His brother's antics had forced Robert to live a life without honor. If whoever had done this were anything like his brother, they wouldn't stop until they got bored or when he and Sparrow were dead.

"Hopefully they think we got caught up in the slide and went over the edge." He reached his hand down to help Sparrow up.

She gripped his palm tightly and smiled as she climbed the rocks. She then threaded her fingers through his and surveyed the scuffs and divots again. He knew he should pull free, but it comforted him to have her tiny fingers intertwined with his. He peeked down at her. Dirt still coated her from head to toes, and her hair was disheveled, but he couldn't remember the last time he saw someone more beautiful.

A strained sound erupted from her lips as she yanked him down off the boulder pile. He scrambled as fast as his big feet could take him and pressed his back against the rocks. His heart pounded in his chest, and he wondered if all this excitement was good for it.

Sparrow pressed her hands against the rocks and hissed in his ear. "There are men down below."

He nodded and motioned for her to stay. He inched up and peeked over the rocks. Two men stood at the trail they'd been on earlier. Though it was hard to distinguish their features, one man wore a dirty red hat.

"That man with the red hat is one of Sterling's men." Her whisper made him flinch and his heart to skip.

He turned to glare at her. "I told you to stay put."

"You told me no such thing."

"Sparrow." Robert elongated her name with a growl.

She looked at him and rolled her eyes. Rocks splattered across his face as the ping of rapid gunfire echoed up the mountain. He pushed her down and covered her with his body.

"Well, there goes the hope that they'd believed we'd gone over." He rubbed the rock bits from his hair with a sigh. "They won't be giving up now." *Especially if it's Sterling.*

"If we get to the horses, we can get away." Sparrow's words were breathless as she ducked when bullets pinged over the rocks again. "They're on the wrong side of the slide. They'll have to find a way to get their horses around it."

"Even then, if Sterling Fitzgerald is involved, they'll be relentless." Robert ran his hand over the back of his neck.

She glanced up at him, her forehead furrowed. "I have an idea."

With that, she took off back toward the horses. Robert followed as the heaviness of impotency settled over him. How was he to ever get out from the deprecation of his past if it kept chasing him down?

## CHAPTER 7

Fear still coated Sparrow's tongue and throat with its thick, choking presence as she led Robert up the treacherous trail her ancestors had abandoned generations ago. Trail was too generous a term as their horses struggled up the steep, rocky mountainside.

Lightning's hoof slipped, and Sparrow's throat tightened even more. Was she right in leading them on this loco path? As bullets had ricocheted off the rock walls, and Robert's face had fallen in defeat at Sterling's name, the ancient path had seemed a God-inspired idea. Now, she questioned the plan with every turn and length they advanced up the mountain.

The only good she could see coming from this harrowing trek would be the lack of followers. They had taken the normal trail for over an hour after they'd gotten back to the horses. They'd finally hit the mile stretch of solid rock that she planned for their escape and veered off of the main thoroughfare. They'd then backtracked through the woods until she had found the abandoned way that even the most knowledgeable tracker would believe to be just a small game trail—if they found it at all.

As a sharp, bitter-cold wind buffeted her face, Sparrow twisted on Lightning's back and peeked at Robert. He looked as miserable as she felt, tucked as tightly into his coat as he could get with his wide-brimmed hat pulled low over his ears. She'd need to find a place to camp soon since the sun was beginning its slip behind the horizon.

She should have had them stay at the place they'd stopped a few hours back. The clearing had had a little stream they'd cleaned up in, watered the horses, and filled canteens with. The grass had provided the horses with a decent meal, and the tall trees would have protected them from the worst of the wind. But her agitated state, and the need to put more ground between them and their attackers, drove her to push on. Robert had only raised an eyebrow at her declaration to mount up. Now, her fear might be the death of them.

*Let not your heart be troubled, neither let it be afraid.* Jesus's words tumbled through her frantic mind. She blinked the sting in her eyes away at the peace that settled upon her heart. Why couldn't that verse have come to her back in the clearing? She silently admonished God, only to quickly beg forgiveness. The verse hadn't come because she had been too caught up in their circumstance. Too focused on the enemy hounding them, than the God guiding them.

*Peace I leave with you.* The calming of the wind quickly followed the first part of the verse. She looked up in amazement as the trail widened to a protected spot on the mountain. It wasn't a cave, more like a deep overhang, but the space was large enough for them to bed down and the horses to have plenty of room.

"Thank You, Lord." She bowed her head as the calm of the Holy Spirit penetrated her soul. "Help me to not lose sight again."

The wind picked back up, but God was true to His Word, leaving peace with her. She pulled Lightning to a stop and dismounted with a sigh. She beamed back at Robert as his feet hit the ground, and he surveyed the area.

"We'll camp here." Sparrow shrugged as she grabbed the hobbles from her pack. "It'll get dark soon."

"That trail is mighty loco during the day. I can't imagine going it at night." Robert uncinched his saddle. "This works as well as any other place."

As he got busy relieving his horse of his gear, Sparrow couldn't help admiring her husband and his easy acceptance of their situation. He didn't try to take charge or undermine her decisions. However, when it came to her protection, he saw to it with a ferocity that both comforted and excited her. Her heart raced just thinking about his body curving over hers as rock shards and bullets had rained down. She chuckled, remembering his disgruntled glare when she'd peeked over the rocks at the men.

She stole a glance at him over Lightning's back as he rubbed his horse down. He winced and rolled his shoulders and neck, and her humor evaporated. Her stomach tightened at the realization that she hadn't even asked if the rockslide had injured him.

She put her forehead on Lightning's side, closing her eyes to control her regret. Robert would worry about her and close up if she blubbered like a baby. Taking a deep breath, she straightened and patted Lightning on the side.

Sparrow sauntered over to where Robert stood looking out over the edge of the mountain. The sun painted the sky brilliant golds, oranges, and deep purples as it disappeared. The mountain range and forest stretched out before their sanctuary. The dark pines deep in the shadow of the mountains wore aspens dotted among them like stars. The trees gave way to jagged crags and white-tipped peaks that towered above them. The wind whistled along the bare slope they stood on and danced down the collar of her coat.

The cry of an eagle carried on the wind. The majestic creature glided through the valley below them before disappearing into its large nest on the top of a dead tree.

"Mounting up with wings as eagles." Robert's voice settled into the pit of her stomach. "I think I like that image."

She peered up at his peaceful expression, her breath leaving her as if the wind had snatched it away. Yes, she hadn't wanted to marry again, the threat of heartache too terrifying to imagine. But she was glad God had arranged for Robert to be hers. Now, she needed to figure out why he didn't feel the same. She'd learned her lesson today, the consequences of her impatience meant a brutally cold night ahead of them, so she'd be patient in her pursuit of his heart, leaning on the peace of God in the meantime.

"But they that wait upon the Lord shall renew their strength," Sparrow quoted the verse from Isaiah glancing back out across the expanse before them. "They shall mount up with wings as eagles; they shall run, and not be weary; and they shall walk, and not faint."

"Yep." He nodded his head as he crossed his arms. "I think I like that a lot."

She smiled before sobering and stepping closer to his side. "Robert, were you hurt in the rockslide?"

"Nah, nothing but a few bumps. It'll keep." His jaw clenched, and she knew he was lying.

"Are you sure?" She ran her hand up his back and felt him recoil.

"Yep." The word squeezed through gritted teeth.

She threaded her fingers through his and pulled him to the gear. "Liar." She tempered the word with a soft smile. "Come, let me look."

He pulled to get free and growled. "Sparrow, I'm fine."

She whirled and placed her fists on her hips. "You will let me look at your back without complaining." She poked her finger into his chest for emphasis.

Robert smirked and rubbed his chest where she'd poked him. "For such a little bitty thing, you sure have a sharp finger."

"And a stubborn will as strong as you are tall." She pointed to where the bedrolls were laid out.

He huffed, his mouth tweaking with a suppressed grin. "Fine, take a peek. I'm telling you, though, it's nothing a few days won't fix."

Sparrow rushed to her pack as he plopped down onto his blankets and started pulling his shirts off. Her hands stalled as she took the healing ointment out of her pack. His well-muscled chest and arms glowed in the waning light like the photographs of the works of Michelangelo she'd seen once in an art book. She'd been embarrassed and enthralled by the statue of David, wondering if a man's muscles could truly be as defined as the statue portrayed. She had her answer in the hard planes and angles of her husband's body.

"Sparrow, the wind's chilly. Think you could pick up the pace?" Robert raised an eyebrow, his neck turning red at her stare.

Quickly averting her eyes, her cheeks flamed hot. She took a deep breath to calm the feeling of lightning coursing through her skin. With a huff, she flipped her pack closed and swallowed the moisture that had pooled in her mouth.

Clearing her throat, she moved toward him. "Why don't you face the mountain wall so I can use the last of the light?"

She kneeled behind him and gasped, her desire draining out of her like rain on rocky ground. Dark circles of varying sizes marred his smooth, tanned skin. Tears pricked her eyes as she noticed thin scars that whipped across his shoulders and back.

"Oh, Robert." The words choked out as she dipped her fingers into the ointment and smeared it over his bruises as gently as she could.

"It's all right, Sparrow. Nothing I haven't felt before."

His low words sliced through her heart. She bit her lip to keep from sobbing, though she couldn't stop the trembling in her fingers. She wondered if he'd open up to her enough to tell her his past. Just as quickly, she wondered if she could handle it if he did.

∼

EXHAUSTION PULLED at Robert's edges, fraying him as the wind whipped across the mountainside in an unrelenting attack. It tugged on his mind, picking apart each thought until all he had were jumbled pieces and moments. How Sparrow could have such calm and peacefulness left him with more questions swirling about his brain, like strings being unraveled from a worn garment and tossed in the breeze. If he didn't sleep, and soon, he wasn't sure if he'd have any brain left.

Slumber proved elusive again tonight, though, with Sparrow moving her bedroll close to his. It was probably better not to sleep anyway, to be on guard against their pursuers. He clenched his hands, trying to stay still as he lay on his side beside his sleeping wife. Her breath blew out on a jagged shiver, pooling frustration in his gut.

He couldn't believe he was running again, following someone else's lead at that. He'd promised himself as he dug William's grave that he wouldn't cower against the enemy and his own doubts anymore. That he'd meet them head on in a way that would please God. He wanted to be like Joshua, who went into the promised land filled with giants and came out saying, "We can conquer them."

He'd done it too.

Found a path God could be proud of.

Robert sighed, shifted, then stilled, not wanting to wake Sparrow. Maybe he should have stood his ground against the attackers instead of running like a coward. It had felt good and right standing between Sparrow and Sterling back in Fryingpan Town, kind of like Elijah of the Bible when he stood with God and called down fire from heaven. Maybe he was a little too much like Elijah, since Robert ran with his tail tucked just like the prophet had. A gust of frigid wind whistled through their camp, causing him to tighten his muscles against a shiver.

"Robert?" Sparrow's words stuttered against her chattering teeth.

"Yeah."

"I'm cold." She scooted up close and buried her face in his chest.

He froze, his heart pounding against his ribs. Sleep definitely was out of the question now. She shivered and placed her hand on his chest, running it up his shoulder and down his arm. The touch trailed fire across his body, scorching the moisture from his mouth. She grabbed his wrist and pulled his arm around her.

"Can you hold me?" The wind carried her words up to his ears.

Her normally strong voice sounded so thready he wanted to agree, but he worried if he held her, he'd never want to let her go. He couldn't do that to her--stitch her into the family curse.

"Please, Robert."

She inched up and laid her head on his arm. He should've used it for a pillow instead of the saddlebag. Then it wouldn't be waiting in invitation for her.

"I'm so cold." Her hot breath tickled his skin, sending heat straight to his gut.

He couldn't do this, couldn't hold her and keep his head on straight. He was already battling the effects of exhaustion and cold, but to add her body curled against his might just incinerate any functioning brain he had left.

Her teeth chattered like a woodpecker rattling against a tree. He wrapped his arms around her and pulled her to him. She sighed and curled her hand around his waist, tucking it between his shirt and skin. She burrowed closer, threading her legs through his.

He'd found a little piece of heaven on the ragged mountainside in the form of his petite wife snuggled up to him, sighing in comfort. Maybe they didn't need to leave the mountain and find her family. He'd be willing to build a house here on the cliffside if it meant he could hold her like this at night. Maybe if they were away from others, the isolation would keep the curse in check. With Sparrow's knowledge and his brute force, together they could create heaven on earth among the soaring eagles and towering cliffs of God's creation.

"Tell me about your family." Her lips brushed against his neck as she spoke, jolting lightning through his skin as her words crumbled the happy picture to rubble.

"Why?" The word squeezed from his chest.

"I want to know you." She slid her hand further around his back as she snuggled closer.

"Trust me, you don't want to know about me."

She pushed back slightly. He could feel her gaze on his face even though the moon offered just a sliver of light to illuminate the night. The wind teased some of her hair from her braid and tickled his cheek with it.

"Yes, Robert, I do."

Maybe it was the steady, low pitch of her voice or the exhaustion chipping away his resolve, but he didn't have the strength to fight her request. Besides, the minute she learned about his family and his past, her hand would find its way back against her own body. She would probably rather suffer curled in a ball against the cold than be close to him. No woman would want to stay close to him when they knew the truth, at least no respectable woman would. That was what he wanted anyway, her distant and uncaring so he wouldn't leave his heart behind with her when he ventured back to his homestead. So why did his throat ache with the words waiting to come forth?

"I didn't—"Robert cleared his throat and tried again. "I didn't have a happy childhood, Sparrow. It's not a pretty bedtime story."

She lay back down upon his arm. "Tell me."

His lips tweaked up at her statement, then settled into a grimace. "My pa worked on the levee loading and unloading riverboats. At least, that's what he did before drinking and gambling took hold of his heart. He'd always had a penchant for drinking and a heavy hand."

Robert inwardly flinched at his early memory of the willow whacking across his legs and back. He'd been about four and remembered crying, asking his pa what he'd done wrong. His pa had told him he'd done nothing wrong, that Sweeneys learned respect by the rod. Robert had realized as he'd lain in his straw-stuffed pallet for a week, his legs so swollen and bruised he couldn't walk, that he wasn't so sure he wanted to be a Sweeney. He'd wondered if there was a way to change families.

"After Pa had gone to work drunk one day and dumped an entire crate of silk fabric in the Mississippi when he stumbled over his own feet, he decided gambling was more his suit anyway. He'd take what little coin my ma made washing laundry and drink and gamble it away. When she'd sneak off to the store to buy food before Pa got home, he'd be furious. One winter, William got sick. He must've been seven, because I had just turned ten. He looked so small in the bed as Ma wiped his forehead with a cloth, lamenting that if we only had some broth to give him, he'd get better.

"That was the day I started stealing from people's

backyards and digging through the alley trash for food. Instead of going to school, I snuck into a yard a ways from our house and lifted a chicken from some person's coop. I'd searched for hours, trying to find a hen house that had plenty so the owners wouldn't notice one measly chicken missing. Ma didn't believe me when I told her one of the neighbors had given it to us, but the look of gratitude and relief in her eyes spurred me on to do it again."

Robert would never forget the fear that had choked him every time he ventured into yards and markets looking for food. He'd been so worried about ending up behind bars that often he'd vomit his small breakfast in the bushes. His ma, knowing his distress, had combed her bony fingers through his hair and told him how brave he was.

"That must've been hard for one so young." Sparrow's soft whisper jolted him back from his ma's soft touch.

"Yeah, well, with Linc off causing a ruckus with the other hoodlums, and Pa drinking and gambling away his time, someone had to take care of Ma and William. Pa would come home proud as a rooster about some trouble Linc had gotten into and how his son had talked his way out of it. I tried to keep away when he was in those moods because he'd often start thrashing me with whatever he could grab ahold of."

She gasped. "Why?"

"Because I was weak, not following in Linc's footsteps, and would never amount to anything."

She scoffed and burrowed closer to him. "Sounds to me like you were the strong one, feeding your family like you did."

Her defense of him had him closing his eyes against the sting of tears that welled there. No one but his ma had ever seen him as anything but bad. Rotten to the core is what the neighbors had said. Robert cleared his throat. Sparrow wouldn't be so quick to defend when he finished.

"So instead of finishing up school, I roamed the streets, searching for food, clothing—anything, really, that my ma might be able to use. After a few years, I tried finding work, but with my family's reputation, no one would hire me. I guess I don't blame them. I wouldn't have hired a Sweeney either.

"When I was fifteen, Pa got himself killed over a game of cards. A few weeks later, Linc got into some trouble that would've probably found him on the end of a rope, so we took off west. Since Linc was eighteen, and I looked that old, he thought we should look for gold and stake a claim. When that proved too much work for Linc, he went back to his cheating and conniving ways, and I went right along with him. Family always sticks together, and he and William were all I had left."

"What happened to your mother?"

He didn't want to tell her, but her soft, tentative voice pulled the thread of his mother free from the past, his words tumbling haltingly out of his mouth. "She died about two months before Pa. A few years before, Pa had started using Ma to pay off his gambling debts, traipsing men in at all hours of the day so she could service them. Pa was all horns and rattles when she up and died from syphilis."

"Oh, Robert."

He talked right over her sympathy. "The doctor said it was the most aggressive case of syphilis he'd ever seen.

The blisters covered her mouth and coated her throat, choking her to death."

Sparrow whimpered in his arms.

Robert kept on talking. "Maybe it was God showing mercy in her quick death. At least, I like to think that's the case. But I'll never forget what she told me on her deathbed—that I needed to break the Sweeney curse that plagued our family with pain and misery. Now, with my brothers both dead, the Sweeney name and curse will die with me."

"I don't understand." She pushed up onto her elbow. A tear glinted in the scant moonlight where it clung to her lashes.

"After I get you to your family safely and get our marriage annulled, I'll go back to my life I'd planned, farming my land to provide food for the mines. If I don't have a family, I stop the curse."

"No, Robert, I—"

"Sparrow, I'm exhausted and done talking, please." He hated the imploring tone in his voice, but he couldn't take any more words—words that wrung him so tight, all life leaked from him.

She wiped the tear from her cheek with a sharp swipe and settled back down. But instead of curling away from him, she melded to him. A soft kiss burned his skin before she sighed, skating her hand inside his coat and wrapping it around his body in a hug. He squeezed his eyes tight to hold in the grief that threatened to spill.

Not grief for his family—that had long dried out—but grief for a life marriage to Sparrow symbolized. A life not just worth living, but abundant in love and maybe even a little joy.

## CHAPTER 8

While Sparrow scanned the tight trail ahead of her, she thought back to the morning. She should pay attention to the horse's footing, but her mind raced with too many thoughts and questions.

She had relished the feel of Robert's arms wrapped tightly around her the next morning, his rhythmic breathing in her hair. She had lain there, wanting to start some shenanigans, as Trapper Dan put it, with her tenderhearted giant, but realizing he needed sleep more. Though, the temptation to lean over, press her lips to his, and run her hand along his muscles had almost overpowered her. The action would have layered more guilt upon his already heavy heart.

Though his shoulders were broad, her husband couldn't possibly hold more guilt.

Sparrow had held back her desire and prayed. Prayed for Robert to recognize the true power of their Living God. She wondered if anyone had ever discipled him, or if the only knowledge of a life rich in God's love was through campfire chats with Trapper Dan and Robert's own reading of the Bible. If he had started at the beginning, she could see how he'd have a skewed understanding of the Word. The Old Testament, while vital to a rich walk with God, was steeped in laws that even the Jews couldn't keep. If all he knew were the laws of God and not the freedom from those laws Jesus had brought, then Robert was still a captive.

He thought that nothing he did or didn't do could break a curse as strong as the one chained around his neck. The more he tried, the tighter it would bind until it eventually suffocated him. She knew the weight guilt had, knew how it could drag one under and drown them. Sure, he had broken free from the prison his father and brother had built around him, only to build a new prison just as confining around himself. She had prayed while lying in his arms watching him sleep and while traveling the rugged mountain pass that God would shake the foundation of Robert's prison so hard the bars burst wide open.

Sparrow glanced around the clearing they were making camp in for the night. A thin waterfall trickled over the edge of the rocks, settling into a pool with dark green shadows and a deep turquoise center that faded to clear in the shallow edges. Chipmunks darted across the ground and up trees, distressing warblers in their nests.

She smiled as the sharp *zeet*, *zeet* of a dipper bird sang over the gurgling water. She surveyed the water, waiting for the small bird to perform its incredible feat. Her patience was rewarded when a dark gray bird swooped over the pool and dived into the water, emerging with droplets dripping from it as it flew to the rocks on the other side of the pond.

Boulders sprouted from the shore, creating a bridge to the deep water. She planned on taking her fishing line and snagging some trout later to smoke for the next day's journey.

She had considered moving on since the sun still had a few hours hanging in the sky, but after almost not finding a place to bed down the previous night, she'd decided stopping wouldn't do any harm. Besides, the more time they had on the trail, the more opportunities she had to get through her husband's thick skull that they were meant to be together.

His words the night before had fractured her heart into so many pieces she was surprised it hadn't been lying in the dirt when they'd finally gotten up and on the road. She'd let it pass, hearing the exhaustion steeping his voice. She had also worried her temper wouldn't hold, drawn out by the pain his words had created.

Sparrow was glad she'd held her tongue as the memory of his soft expression when he had awoken and the way his lips had parted slightly as his gaze had traced her face and landed on her mouth. Lands alive, she'd forgotten to breathe as his hand had skimmed up her back and then tucked a loose strand of hair behind her ear.

Her heart had shrunk when his expression had shuttered, and he'd sat up faster than a bullfrog on a lily pad, almost flinging her to her feet in the process. She could've let his lack of attention or the limited conversation the rest of the day bother her, but she chose instead to focus on that one precious moment and the looks she caught him sneaking when he thought she wasn't paying attention.

With their rabbit dinner roasting over the fire and

camp set up, Sparrow wove aspen branches to smoke the trout on while she watched Robert. He dug through his saddlebag and pulled out his Bible. Striding with purpose to a flat boulder next to the pond and sitting, he heaved a big sigh before opening the book.

She finished weaving, checked dinner, and ambled over to his rock. She climbed on top of it and sat with her legs hanging over the water. His forehead scrunched. She chose to believe it was in confusion over the ancient text and not her arrival.

"It's honorable for you to want to read the Bible like you do." She tossed a golden aspen leaf into the water and watched it slowly float away.

"How else am I supposed to know what God expects of me? It's not like we live in a place that has a church, at least not yet." Exasperation tinged his low tone.

"True." She tossed another leaf into the pond. "It's hard, though, to read it from cover to cover."

He sighed and put the book on his lap. "Just how do you suggest I do it, Sparrow, since I'm obviously doing it wrong."

She turned from the water to look at him, a knot forming in her stomach. "That's not what I meant." She reached over and placed her hand on his. "It's amazing that you haven't given up. I would've hit Numbers and called it quits."

A low chuckle emitted from him as he shook his head. "That section was definitely a handful."

"Can I tell you something Dan once told me?" she asked with hesitance, praying that God would soften his heart. When he shrugged, she scooted closer, taking the Bible from his hand and flipping it open. "The Bible is a collection of books, and within that collection are different styles, like history, poetry, prophecy, and letters to name a few. But because it's a collection of books, we don't have to read it from front to back. Does that make sense?"

"Yeah, I guess it does." He ran his hand through his hair.

"I was confused, not sure where to start learning about God." She smiled as she ran her hand over the leather cover already worn from daily use. "He suggested that I start with the book of John, because that was one of the four books accounting Jesus's life. Then Acts, since that is the book describing how the first Christians spread the Good News of Jesus. After that he said I should either read the letters of John or Ephesians. It surprised me when he said this because all of these books are in the back of the Bible." She looked up at Robert and chuckled. "I challenged him about that, arguing that you couldn't read the end of a book before the beginning. He said I was free to read however I wanted, but to truly understand the love of God and His forgiveness, learning about Jesus first would make it easier to understand the Old Testament."

"But how are you to follow all the rules God lays out in the front of the Bible if you don't even read it?" Robert took back the Bible and opened it to Deuteronomy.

"Living a life for God isn't about all the rules we have to follow. God freed us from all that when Jesus died on the cross and forgave our sins."

"I understand that. I accepted a life following Jesus and the sacrifice that comes with that."

She snorted and rubbed her hand down her face. "Then why are you concerned about following the laws?

Why haven't you accepted that Jesus doesn't expect you to break your family curse? Only He can do that."

"Haven't you read the front of the Bible? It's full of people who veered from God's plan and ended up perishing, pits opening and swallowing them whole. If I want to make it to heaven, I have to stay in control, to walk the narrow path to the pearly gates. Only then will I be allowed in." Robert stood and paced away from the rock, but not before she heard his faint whisper. "Maybe."

Her throat throbbed and face flushed with heat as she jumped from the rock and stomped toward him. "Robert Sweeney, you may understand it up in that big head of yours, but you haven't accepted the forgiveness of God in here." She poked his chest. "You've been in darkness for so long, you don't know how to let go of it. First John says that if we walk in the light, as He is in the light, have fellowship with one another, then the blood of Jesus Christ his Son cleanseth us from all sins. It doesn't say if I work really hard and follow all the rules, my sins are forgiven. No matter how good we are, we can never earn forgiveness. It says that if we confess our sin, He is faithful and just to forgive us our sins, and cleanse us from all unrighteousness. Not just the sin of that moment or day, but all of our filth, Robert. You don't have to keep wallowing in it. Jesus said that 'the thief cometh not, but for to steal, and to kill, and to destroy: I am come that they might have life, and that they might have it more abundantly.'"

She threw her arms into the air. "Why are you letting the devil steal your life away? Why are you allowing him to bind you to a curse God has already freed you from? You did it, Robert. You already fulfilled your promise to your mother when you turned from darkness and walked toward the light of God. Stop allowing the devil to reign over you. God wants you to have life abundantly, and I want you to have that life with me."

His head flinched back slightly. "Wh—What?"

Sparrow dashed away the angry tears that coursed down her hot cheeks and growled in frustration. "I'm going fishing. Watch dinner."

She stomped away, snatched up her fishing kit she'd strung up earlier, and ventured out on the boulders to the center of the pond. Anger tightened her ribs, putting pressure on her core. Anger at Robert for his rejection of her and oblivion to her feelings toward him. But mostly anger at herself for railing at him. She dropped her sack on the largest boulder, fished a cricket out of her pocket she'd caught earlier for bait, and hooked it onto her line. Tossing the hook into the water, she plopped onto the rock as tears fell down her cheeks and pleadings for forgiveness tumbled from her lips.

∽

ROBERT LEANED against his saddle propped behind him on the ground, reading by the light of the fire. He hadn't wanted to believe what Sparrow had said to him. Had been shocked by how angry she'd been. Her anger hadn't been like any anger he'd ever witnessed before, puzzling him to no end.

As he'd stood by the fire, checking the rabbit while watching her dash her hand over her face as she fished, he realized her outrage hadn't been at him. No, it seemed to come more out of pain for him.

He couldn't comprehend her anguish for him, but he did understand that he wanted the life she described—a life out of the darkness. So, with shaky, cold fingers, he'd turned to the book of John and read. Quick off the draw, he'd been hit with a God far different from the one Robert had constructed in his mind. This new God talked about the law given by Moses, but that grace and truth came from Jesus.

Could it be that Robert couldn't understand the law until he understood the truth of Jesus? He'd devoured the words, sitting long after dinner had been served and eaten. Long after Sparrow had smoked her trout she'd caught and turned in for bed. Long after the owls hooted in the trees and the coyotes yipped in the distance.

Robert would be the first to admit there was a lot he didn't quite grasp, but there was something he noticed repeated over and over again that only a fool would miss. The love of God poured out upon the very pages of John. Not rules and edicts, but Jesus healing men and women of their spiritual and physical ailments with little more than them calling out to Him.

Is this what Sparrow meant, this being able to see after stumbling around in the darkness of sin? His eyes glossed over, and pain ached in his chest. He had read that Jesus was the light of the world, that whoever followed him would not walk in darkness, but have the light of life. Robert was tired of making his own way, of the demons that seemed to claw at his back and pull him down no matter what he did.

He flipped to First John and read, trying to find the verse Sparrow had spoken. His eyes slammed to a stop at six small words at the end of verse four. *That your joy may be full.* Had he ever felt joy, even after accepting Christ?

Robert stared at those words and shook his head. No, he'd only ever felt pressure and condemnation. Jesus had said there was no condemnation in Him, so why was Robert still holding on to it? He wanted that joy that came from God. He wanted peace, knowing he belonged in the light. He didn't want to keep himself separate from others, but wanted to fellowship with them and with Christ. His gaze landed on Sparrow—on where she'd laid her bedroll next to his, even though he hadn't said a word to her since their argument. He wanted a life abundant, a life walking hand in hand with her on the path God laid before them.

His breath quickened as warmth built in his gut. He stared up at the stars shining brilliantly down on him, seeming to sparkle with encouragement. He tried to take a deep breath but couldn't.

"Lord, I don't want to be in the dark anymore. Please, Lord, I can't." He swallowed the lump in his throat. The stars blurred as tears burned his eyes. "I can't carry this weight. Please, please help me. Forgive me. Take this curse that has dragged my family to the depths of hell. I don't want it to drag me too. I don't want it to darken my life with fear. I want life abundant. I want a life in You, Lord."

A warm wind swirled through the camp as Robert's heart burst with heat and love he'd never before experienced. A lightness lifted his shoulders and tingling surged from his head and spread to his fingers and toes. His breath shuddered out as his chin collapsed to his chest, and he heaved silent sobs he couldn't control. When all the years of pain had leaked down his shirt, a sense of calm covered him.

He took a deep breath and lifted his eyes back to the stars. "Thank you, Lord."

Robert ran his hand over the Bible one last time before tucking it into his saddlebag. As if floating on clouds, he glided over to his bedroll. When Sparrow rolled over and hesitantly eased her hand on his chest, Robert only paused a moment before he pulled her close, grasping tight to the promise he'd heard in her words—a future bright in the light of the Lord.

## CHAPTER 9

Robert inhaled freedom deeply within his chest, bottling it up within his lungs. He closed his eyes and exhaled hope. He'd woken with Sparrow snuggled close and his body relaxed and refreshed for the first time since he could remember. He couldn't even dredge up the nausea that had sat like a geyser in his stomach since they'd left Fryingpan Town. Sparrow's eyebrows had risen, and her mouth quirked several times while they broke camp and headed out.

He was still quiet, not speaking much since that was just his way, so he wondered what kind of expression he wore for her to sneak peeks at him like he would sprout wings and fly. With how light he felt, he wouldn't be surprised if he did. *Thank You, Lord.*

A light breeze whistled along the steep mountain trail he wasn't even sure goats would travel, teasing in his coat and tangling in his hair. He lifted his arms and stretched out his hands, tipping his head back to the sun. His fingers on one hand skimmed the rock cliff jutting up the mountain. With the wind rushing along his arms, swirling his body, and the sun warming his face, he wondered if this was how eagles felt—free from darkness dragging them down, chaining them to the earth.

"Robert, what are you doing?" The wind whooshed Sparrow's laugh to him.

He pulled the joyful sound in, allowing it to vibrate to the depths of his soul. A slow smile curved upon his face, the feeling foreign and wonderful.

"I'm mounting up with wings like an eagle." He lowered his arms and gazed at her, twisting on her horse to look back at him. "I haven't gotten to that part yet, but the image of a beautiful warrior princess once doing just that stuck with me. I had to try it for myself." He winked.

Sparrow's eyes widened and her cheeks pinked like primrose flowers before she turned forward. His smile stretched larger. Had he ever flirted with a woman before? He couldn't remember, and now was glad he hadn't, reserving all his amorous words for her.

"But they that wait upon the Lord shall renew their strength; they shall mount up with wings as eagles; they shall run, and not be weary; and they shall walk, and not faint." Her strong voice echoed across the valley.

Robert's chest tightened, and he blew out the feeling. He knew without a doubt that God had renewed Robert's strength. He felt a bit like Samson must've after his hair grew back. In fact, since becoming a Christian, Robert now realized he had an awful lot in common with the hero of Judges.

Like Samson, he had relied more on his own strength than God. It was probably why he had always felt so exhausted. Yet, waiting on the Lord and letting go of

Robert's control had renewed him. He just prayed his story ended better than Samson's had.

His gaze lingered on Sparrow, her braid swinging with the horse's steps. He wanted to unplait the dark strands and see if they were as silky as they looked. He had wanted to claim the promise he'd seen written across her face that morning with a kiss, but his throat had dried with uncertainty. He'd cleaned up camp like always, wishing he'd just dived into the hope shining from her eyes.

Robert was trying hard not to worry about what kind of future he had with her. God had brought them together, but would God also provide the means to keep them together?

Robert had been so focused on not thinking about having a family, that now the possibility of a wife and children expanded his heart until it felt three times larger in his chest. A million questions raced through his head—where would they live? Would the government allow them to live where they wanted? Would she change her mind when they got to her people? Robert slammed the doubt from his mind and looked out over the rocky mountaintop. He would just wait upon the Lord's leading.

His eyes narrowed as she led them on a slope so steep, he wasn't sure how the loose rocks and dirt stayed put. "Sparrow, be caref—"

The primal scream filled his ears a split second before his horse slipped from under him. Stomach in his throat, he grappled with the saddle-horn and tried to free his feet from the stirrups as his horse's body slammed into the rock slope rising beside the trail. Pain spiked up his leg, closing his throat.

The horse landed against the trail, pinning Robert to the powdery dirt. His head knocked against the unrelenting mountain, and stars exploded before his face. Acid filled his throat as the horse slid off the cliff with Robert still beneath him. He clawed at the loose dirt and rocks that mocked him in their instability.

His eyes darted to Sparrow, her mouth open in a scream he couldn't hear. A terrified shriek and sickening thud of the horse tumbling to its death filled him. The relief of weightlessness hit him.

*God, help me!*

Desperate, he dug his fingers and legs into whatever surface he could find purchase, only to come up short. The mountain gave way beneath him, and he was sliding off the edge.

His hand snagged on a sharp, jutting rock. He clung to it. His fingers were slick with blood, and his grip loosened. Reaching up with his other hand to find a hold, he yelped when a lariat landed around his arm. He followed the rope to its end where tiny Sparrow held it wrapped around a boulder. His hands turned to ice.

"No, Sparrow, don't." He choked on the words as they pushed loose.

"Find a better grip." Her neck bulged with the effort of holding him.

He kicked his legs, frantic to find purchase and relieve her of his weight. "Let go! I'll just pull you over with me."

She speared him with a determined stare. "Fight your way up, Robert Sweeney, because I'm not letting you go—not ever. Even if that means I go to the depths of the valley with you. Family always sticks together!"

Tears blurred his vision. Though his fingers slipped

with each movement, he gripped them tighter and reached with the other hand. A solid-looking rock was embedded just out of reach. He tried again, his arm pulling tight in the socket as Sparrow yanked on the rope. Two inches, that's all he needed, two inches. He placed his feet upon the cliff wall and pushed. His fingertips brushed the rock as his feet slipped out from under him. A yell ripped from him as only two bloody fingers held him and Sparrow between life and death.

"God, help!" He groaned as he pulled himself back up, planting his feet on the cliff wall again.

His legs fully straightened, but his fingers only grazed the solid rock. He closed his eyes. *I trust You, Lord.* With a howl, he leaped, for a moment soared, up the mountain and clenched his hand solidly around the rock. He groaned and pulled himself up to reach his other hand onto the trail. His arms shook, and he pushed his strength to its limits as he climbed the rest of the way onto solid ground. With a shudder, he rolled onto his back, tears streaming down his face.

Sparrow crawled over to him, her chest heaving in great sobs. She collapsed onto him and hugged him tightly. He pulled her close, his arms still shaking from exertion. She pushed up, wiped her arm across her eyes, and leaned over his face.

"Are you all right?" Her hair spilled from her braid where it hung over her shoulder.

He pushed his hand through her hair, cupped the back of her head and pulled her to him. His heart exploded with the touch of her lips, and he deepened the kiss. It wasn't the tender kiss he had imagined giving her, but one of desperation, love, and a bit of fright. He kissed her for all the lost times he'd wanted to claim her lips and for all the hopeful thoughts of years of loving her in the future.

He slowed the kiss and pulled her so that her head lay on his shoulder. His heart beat erratically in his chest, and he needed to catch his bearings before he slid right off the mountain again.

"You shouldn't have done that, Sparrow." His voice sounded like he was churning stones.

She pushed up and stared into his face. "I couldn't lose you, Robert, not when I just found you."

"I—" His throat burned in the back of it, and he cleared away the emotion. "I love you, Sparrow. I don't understand what God was doing when He brought you into my life, but I'm glad He did."

She smiled and kissed him gently before pushing up. "I love you too, Robert. Now, let's get off this loco mountain so we can start living again."

He smiled and pushed up to sit with a groan. Now that the danger had passed, his entire body radiated pain. He peered over the side of the cliff and shuddered at the sickening drop. He thanked God for helping him and pulled his feet under him to stand. With a hiss, he collapsed back onto his rear and leaned against the mountain.

"Robert?" She knelt beside him, her eyebrows drawn together as she ran her hand across his shoulder and behind his neck.

He could really get used to her comfort. "My leg." He pointed with his chin, grabbing his thigh. "It hurts something fierce."

She bit her lower lip, looked down at his leg, then over to her horse. A sharp wind whipped across the mountain, whining a mournful sound as it blew. She shook her head and focused on him.

"I want to get off this mountain before I look at it." She cupped her small hand on his cheek, the caring touch that mended the fragments of his heart. "Let's get you on Lightning, then I'll lead her off this death trap. When we're out of danger, we both can ride."

"Sparrow—"

"No arguments, husband. Not until I look at your leg."

He liked the word husband falling from her lips. He tugged her to him and kissed her again, her lips tasting of sweat, dirt, and sass. Sighing, he placed his forehead on hers.

"All right, wife, no arguing."

She kissed him softly one more time before leveraging under his shoulder to help him up. He might never be able to admit just how much help he'd needed mounting, but, once the need to vomit had eased, she patted him on the leg and led Lightning down the mountain. While life had no guarantees of ease and comfort, with the love of God and the love of Sparrow, Robert realized he'd found that abundant joy God talked about.

~

Sparrow eased Lightning into a clearing along a small creek. Aspens clapped quietly above them as their gold leaves fluttered in the breeze. No matter how often she travelled the mountains, their beauty and variety never ceased to amaze her. The top of the ridge bore signs of winter's approach, but down here, in this tranquil valley, autumn's splendor still reigned.

The arduous trek down the mountain had seemed too slow, especially with Robert injured. She had prayed for God's patience whenever the desire to rush had overwhelmed her. Between those prayers and ones for Robert's leg, she hadn't stopped petitioning the Lord since Robert went over the cliff.

A cold rush of fear slid over her skin with the memory of the horse's scream and Robert's face. His determination not to take her over the edge with him still cut to her heart. Fool man. Thank God, her husband had come to his senses and not given up.

He shifted behind her with a groan. She admired how tough he was. He hadn't shown much pain past that first admittance he was injured. In fact, if it wasn't for the way his breath hitched now and then, she wouldn't know he was hurt. He'd do well among the men of her tribe, and if not, then she'd leave with him to somewhere else.

Somewhere they could live together in peace.

"We stay here," she whispered, not wanting to disturb the serene surroundings.

Robert grunted his acknowledgement but pulled her back tighter against his chest. Riding double had its benefits. As he deeply exhaled, his breath tickled the skin on her neck. His lips followed where his breath left off, tracing a trail from just below her ear down.

"Mmm, maybe we just get a pack mule instead of another horse." His chest rumbled with his words, causing her stomach to riot like trout on a hook.

"No. You need a horse." Sparrow leaned back against him.

"I don't know. I think I like this much better than

riding alone." He shifted, then groaned. "Then again, it's rough on the backside."

Sparrow patted his uninjured leg and slid off Lightning's back. "Come, husband."

"Anything you say, wife." Robert winked at her.

Winked!

Between his kisses and flirting, she wasn't sure what to make of him. Maybe she should have pushed him off the mountainside earlier? Might have relieved her of days of frustration.

His muscles shook as he swung his leg over Lightning's rump. When his face blanched whiter than new snow, Sparrow wrapped her arm tighter around him. If he passed out, she didn't want him injuring his leg worse.

He leaned his body over the horse's back and sucked in air like he'd just run down the mountain instead of riding. She prayed his leg wasn't broken. The way his horse had pinned Robert against the rock, the possibility of many snapped bones was high.

She scanned the area for resources. The trees stood tall and straight, bundled together close to the water like a bunch of old women gossiping over chores. If need be, she could build a structure among them to protect her and Robert while he healed. The creek ran fast and clear, and trout darted beneath the dark overhang on the opposite bank.

Though winter approached, it wouldn't bury them for at least a month at this lower elevation. She could even hunt for mule deer or elk and tan the hides for added protection and warmth. Nodding, she rubbed Robert's back. Yes, they could make a good camp here, maybe even a home.

"Okay. I'm ready." Robert huffed, his color not so sickly.

Her husband truly was one tough man. Her lips twitched into a smile. She liked that.

He draped his arm across her shoulder. With more weight on her than she knew her gentle mountain man wanted, they made their way to a downed tree. She used her foot to brush away rocks and sticks, then turned to Robert.

"Before you sit, you need to take your pants off."

Bright red, like cardinal feathers, rushed up his neck and into his cheeks. For a man with such a hard reputation, his blushing made her chuckle.

"Okay." He cleared his throat.

"Yes. It is okay." She tipped her head to the side. "Even if we weren't married, I would need your pants off to doctor your wound. Unless you want me to cut the pant leg?"

What a waste of good clothing that would be.

"No, it's fine." He cleared his throat again and dropped his pants.

She rolled her eyes. It wasn't like he didn't have long johns on. Just when she thought he was comfortable around her, he went and showed his lack of experience with women. No worries. She was determined to heal him of that as well.

After lowering him to the ground, she took out her knife and sliced a cut up the leg of his undergarments. She could always sew that back together if he insisted on wearing them. His leg, while swollen, didn't have any bulges indicating a fracture.

"Good. Still straight." She smiled up at him. "I'll need to press on the sides to check for smaller breaks."

Robert gritted his teeth and nodded once. Starting at his thigh, she pressed along his leg, feeling for shifting bones. Robert's only sign of discomfort was his fingers clenching the grass beneath him.

When she reached his foot and felt each bone, she sighed in relief that nothing moved out of place. "Nothing's broken."

"That's good." He relaxed his fingers from the grass and wiped the back of his hand across his sweating forehead.

"I'll get a fire going and brew you some willow bark tea, then after I set up camp, I'll make you a poultice. You'll be bruised, but you'll live." She kissed him, relief flooding her that his injuries weren't bad.

She'd take care of him, make him rest a day even if it drove him loco. Standing slowly, she breathed in the loamy scent of the changing season and let her shoulders relax. Her village couldn't be more than two or three days away. Taking time to heal wouldn't hurt.

She peeked back at Robert. Though his stare was hazy with pain, his eyes tracked every move she made. Joy filtered through her like the sun through the golden leaves. No, taking time here alone wouldn't hurt one bit.

## CHAPTER 10

Sparrow encouraged Lightning over the rise, wondering if this mountaintop would reveal the flatlands that led to Chief Ouray's village. Part of her hoped for a rest from travel, but a larger part of her prayed for more mountains to cross. The last two days since Robert had almost fallen off the cliff and out of her life had been some of the most incredible she'd ever remembered. Not only had he held her close and showered her with kisses, but they'd also had long conversations of their pasts and dreams for the future. When she'd voiced her reluctance to leave her people during this chaotic time, surprise flushed through her body with a pleasant tingling when he had said he would stay with her people if that was what she wanted. When she'd asked about his beautiful cabin, he had just shrugged and replied that he could build another one.

She sighed and leaned back against him as Lightning plodded the last few feet to the ridge. Robert pulled her tighter up against him and nuzzled his lips against her neck. They crested the ridge, and she gasped. In one swift movement, Robert's arm tightened around her, and his gun swished from his holster.

She patted his arm before motioning before them. "Look, Robert."

Just beyond the mountain, the rocky slopes gave way to red and tan desert. She could see the trail to the village past the gulley before them. Though the sun was getting low in the sky, an energy rushed through her to see her people. She silently chided herself and rubbed her slicked hands on her tunic. It would take the rest of the day to get down the mountains, and most likely another day or two to get to the village. Not to mention that she wasn't even sure her people would still be there. The government could've come and taken them away.

She stifled the beam that spread across her face and turned to Robert. "Let's get down the mountain and camp at the base. Then tomorrow we'll head out early and make it to the trail."

"However many days you want to keep me in the wilderness with you is fine by me." He deliberately raised his eyebrows, and his gaze stopped on her lips.

"You rogue." She swatted him, causing him to chuckle that low, delicious sound that caused warmth to bubble in her gut.

"Since we have this amazing view, I believe I'll stretch my legs before we head down." He swung off the back of Lightning's rump, only slightly wincing when he landed.

Relief had rushed away the worry when they'd been able to stop and examine his leg. Surely God had been protecting him, for while his ankle was sore and the leg was black and blue, no serious damage had been done.

Robert bent his legs and did a little dance-like step that made Sparrow giggle as she swung down.

"I sure miss my saddle," he said for the hundredth time. "I don't know how you do it. I feel every cotton-picking bone in that horse's back jabbing with every step."

"Well, don't worry. When we get to my people, we'll barter for a horse with a proper saddle for you." She leaned into his side, wrapping her arm around his back.

"I don't know what with. All my money and belongings tumbled down that cliff." He sighed and draped his arm across her shoulder.

"Don't worry, Robert. We'll figure out something."

He kissed the top of her head. "That we will, my little warrior princess. That we will."

A herd of deer bounded in the trees below them, their tawny bodies jumping and dashing this way and that. She scanned the woods behind the animals, trying to find what had startled them. A flash of color hinted in her peripheral, but when she turned to find it, nothing but forest greeted her. She shook off the chill that raced down her back with a roll of her shoulders. Since starting this trek, she'd been jumping at shadows. More than likely a bear or mountain lion had startled the deer. She'd have to think about that when she found their camp tonight.

"I've never been this far west before." Robert's hushed tone had her peering up at him. He released a slow, deep breath. "The desert is beautiful with its reds and browns all swirling together."

She liked that description. "I've always loved this area. While the Yampah has its hot springs and jutting mountains, the rolling hills, hidden crevices and bunched-up boulders can be just as fascinating."

He peered over his shoulder and whistled, turning them as one to gaze behind them. The mountain range marched like giants behind them, new snow on the tops of the tallest. The magnitude of what they'd just crossed sent goosebumps to slide along her neck.

"'Thy righteousness is like the great mountains; thy judgements are a great deep; O Lord, thou preservest man and beast.'" Sparrow gazed up at Robert as he took a deep breath and continued. "Thank You, Lord for preserving us. Thank You for loving me despite my tainted path." His Adam's apple bobbed as he swallowed and peered down at her. "Thank You for sending me Sparrow to holler in my face and wake me up to Your truth."

Sparrow's mouth dropped open with a gasp. He caught the gasp with his kiss, and she wasn't so offended anymore. As she wrapped her arms around his neck and he lifted her off her feet, she sent up her own prayers of thanksgiving.

∽

A BEAD of sweat rolled down from Robert's hair and dripped off his cheek. The heat of the lower elevation had him wishing for his saddlebags to stow his coat in. In some ways, he wished he could turn the horse around and find a nice spot in the mountains to build them a cabin and keep Sparrow all to himself. Or maybe just find a place not so far to camp for a week or two longer, letting winter decide when to push on.

He shook his head at his thoughts. Staying in the mountains would be a green hand thing to do. Only someone inexperienced would allow their heart to dictate their survival. He knew a large part of his reluctance stemmed from his fear of what Sparrow's people would think of him. Would they accept him? What would he do if her band didn't? Despite what he had first thought when starting this journey, he couldn't leave her. If the tribe refused him, Sparrow and he would figure it out, maybe head farther west into Oregon or Washington.

Another bead of sweat ran down his face, making him wonder how it could be so hot in fall. "How are the winter's dow—"

Sparrow fell off the horse, dragging him with her as a shot pinged off the rock behind him. Lightning reared before taking off back up the trail. He scrambled toward safety as bullets buzzed past him like a swarm of angry bees, kicking dirt into his face where they impaled the ground beside him. He growled as gunfire exploded the mesquite tree he'd hidden behind, splinters biting into his face.

He frantically scanned the area until his eyes landed on Sparrow tucked behind a cluster of rocks on the opposite side of the trail. She nocked an arrow into her bow and met his gaze. How she'd managed to grab her weapon and yank him off the horse while falling herself put a new level of amazement on his already soaring opinion of her. She motioned for him to cover her. All breath left his lungs, and his head spun. As he glared and shook his head, she spun the opposite way and disappeared around the rocks.

With his heart in his throat and incoherent prayers racing through his head, Robert started firing at the group of boulders the drygulcher's shots came from and raced to another bunch of mesquite in the opposite direction of

Sparrow. Robert had to find better cover than the narrow, twisting trunks barely bigger than his thigh. A yelp turned his head in time to see a dirty red hat flying from the short, skinny man from the landslide. The man landed face first in the dirt and didn't move.

Shots fired toward where Sparrow must be. Robert had to get to a better position. With their focus on her, he dashed across an empty space and climbed up a jumble of boulders. A head popped up in the rocks thirty yards ahead of him, and he shot. The thump and drop of the man from his sight pushed acid up his throat.

"You'll pay for that, Sweeney!" Sterling's angry voice assaulted Robert a second before the mesquite he'd been hiding in exploded in a barrage of bullets.

He smiled with slight satisfaction that they didn't know his location. The advantage had momentarily turned. He steadied himself on the rock and waited for someone to expose their hiding hole. An arrow sliced through the air, followed by a pained yell. The other man from the rockslide stood, an arrow sticking from his shoulder, and raised his pistol toward Sparrow's location. Robert shot. The man spun with the impact and fell out of sight.

As the report of the shot faded, an eerie silence blanketed the area. Robert held his breath, cursing his thumping heart making it difficult to hear. He scurried down the boulders as quietly as he could, cringing when his boots scuffed against the rocks. The sound resonated loudly and tellingly in the quiet. He skirted the boulders and darted to a stand of mesquite twisted together. He took a deep breath in and exhaled silently. Finally, having a second to think, he lifted his eyes to the sky and silently begged for help. The sound of a scuffle pushed his heart into his throat and had him assessing where it came from.

"Sweeney!" Sterling's yell cut through the air, and Robert swallowed the bile that rushed to his mouth. "I've got your savage."

Robert peered through the leaves, heat flushing his body at the sight of a disheveled Sterling holding Sparrow in front of him. Blood trickled down her cheek from a gash on her temple. Sterling's face held his customary smirk as he pressed his gun to her head. Ice and heat warred for purchase in Robert's blood, pulling in his gut and making his heart sluggish. Sterling yanked her head to the side and licked up her cheek. Red-hot anger flashed from Robert's gut and into his hands and head, evaporating his cold fear.

"She tastes good, Sweeney. I might just have to drag her back with me like I planned before this whole thing started."

Robert exploded from his covering, his Colt cocked and aimed at Sterling's head. Sterling ducked behind Sparrow like the coward he was. Robert narrowed his eyes and growled.

"Let her go, Sterling. Your fight is with me."

"My fight has never been with you, Robert. You're nothing but dung, a filthy leech on society just like your pa."

Robert chuckled without humor. "Then why'd you chase us for days across the mountains? How many nights did you hole up here, waiting for us to arrive? If I'm nothing but dung, then what are you so afraid of? Why not just let us leave?"

"No one crosses me and lives. You of all people should

know that." Sterling's allusion to their crossed past made Robert flinch. "Does your little squaw know about your past? Does she know how you turned your back on a girl as she called out for help?" Robert peeked at Sparrow's face, who gazed encouragingly at him. Sterling inhaled, closing his eyes as he wet his lips. "My first taste of a struggling woman turned into quite a thriving business for me. Do you know how much money I'm worth? How I've provided what tempts men with great success? You made that possible, Robert, by turning the other way and not going to the authorities."

Robert blinked the moisture from his eyes as a sharp pain burst within his heart. Félicie Tremblay's innocent face, twisted in horror and pain, had haunted him for the last ten years. He could see her blonde hair torn from her bun, and her overly bright blue eyes stared at him often when he closed his own for sleep. The stuttering tremors of her voice calling to him for help often jolted him awake.

"Robert, love, you are cleansed." Sparrow's strong words penetrated his haze. He peered at her. "Your past no longer has power over you."

A deep sense of truth rushed into his tight chest. The lightness he'd experienced on the mountain rushed back in him with a clarity of mind. He couldn't do anything about the past. God had already taken care of that when He forgave Robert of his sins. Robert narrowed his eyes on Sterling, vowing the wretched man would not strip Robert of his future.

A slight fluttering of Sparrow's fingers before she slid a thin blade from her tunic momentarily widened his eyes. She had a plan. He braced himself.

"Give it up, Sterling. This isn't what God wants from your life." He prayed Sterling would listen.

"God? What does a Sweeney know of God?"

"God saved me. He can save you, too, Sterling. Please, don't do this." He adjusted his grip on his Colt.

Sterling sneered and tightened his hold on her neck. "I'll save myself, like always."

Robert's senses tunneled to Sterling with intense focus. A twist of Sterling's lip. His eyes narrowed. The smell of sagebrush and gunpowder on the breeze. Sterling moved the gun from Sparrow's head toward Robert.

Sunlight glinted off of Sparrow's knife as she dropped her blade into Sterling's foot. His howl of pain pierced the air an instant before she lunged away from him. As Sterling whipped his gun up toward Robert, Robert shot and dove sideways, crashing onto his side. Sterling collapsed to the ground, the terror of the moment blowing away with the chilled breeze.

A yell brought his attention to Sparrow, who crawled through the Colorado desert dirt toward him. He reached for her, but his arm didn't work. His eyebrows lowered and his mind muddled as he peered down. Blood ran the length of his coat from his shoulder. His head went light, and he worried he'd ruin his heroic rescue by fainting.

Who was he kidding?

Sparrow's quick action saved them. He probably would still be cowering behind the mesquite, figuring out a way to run if it hadn't been for his wife. His wife, who insisted on running toward danger instead of away.

Robert paused on that thought. Him being a coward may have been true in the past, but he hadn't cowered today.

No, together, he and Sparrow had stood in the face of fear. He smiled as Sparrow reached him, relishing the new life and strength he'd found along the Colorado mountain trail.

∼

"Well, at least life won't be boring." Robert's whisper caught on the wind.

"What?" Sparrow asked, her tongue clucking in concern. Had her husband lost his mind?

"Nothing. Just commenting on how life with a danger-loving woman won't be without its excitement, is all." He closed his eyes as he clenched his teeth.

"Oh, hush, Robert." She swatted his leg, heat sweeping through her cheeks. "You know we had to take care of those polecats if we wanted to make it out alive."

She flattened her lips and tongue and issued a shrill, loud whistle. His head jerked. He placed his hand to his forehead, and his skin looked blotchy. She hoped he didn't lose his breakfast.

She gently pulled his coat off and examined his wound. It was bleeding profusely, but the bullet had gone all the way through. Pity all the blood would probably stain his coat. She shook her head and *tsked*.

Robert sucked in shallow breaths. He grabbed a lock of her hair and pulled it gently through his fingers. "I'm sorry, Sparrow. I'm sorry I'm not going to be able to have that life with you." His voice thickened.

"What are you talking about?" Her chest went hot with anger. She didn't just fight off four sidewinders to have her husband leave her.

"Your face … my wound must be bad." He swallowed. "I wish we coul—"

"Oh, for Pete's sake, Robert. You aren't dying." She rolled her eyes and stood as Lightning trotted into the clearing.

"I'm … I'm not?" His voice trembled.

"No, Robert. It's a clean shot." She unhooked her bag from Lightning's back and shook her head as she knelt back by Robert. "I was lamenting the stains on your coat. I'm not sure I can get the blood out."

He flopped onto his back with a wince. "Okay. That's good."

She smiled softly as she worked on cleaning the wound. She took a deep breath, thankful her heart no longer beat rapidly in her throat, choking her. After packing the bullet hole with a clean cloth, she sat back and shook her head.

"We're going to have to set up camp. I need a fire to sterilize the needle and thread, and I need to bury those men."

"Sterilize?"

"I learned from Orlando this summer the importance of using clean tools." She pushed to her feet, exhaustion weighing her muscles and making the action hard, and started gathering wood for a fire. "If the needle and thread are dirty, the wound could get infected." She dropped the wood and shielded her eyes with her hand. "I wonder if any of those men have whiskey in their saddlebags?"

"You taking up drinking?" He raised his eyebrows.

"No. It will clean your wound and the tools better than boiled water." He blanched at her words, and she inwardly chuckled. "I'm going to go find their horses and bring them over here."

Robert pushed up with a groan and stood shakily. "I'll go check the men. See if any are just wounded and need help."

"Robert, rest. I can do that." She pressed on his uninjured shoulder, trying to get him to sit back down.

He took her hand, examining her fingertips before kissing them. "Sparrow, we do this life together. The good and the bad. I'm not just gonna lie around and let you check dead bodies, make camp, and take care of me. What kind of husband do you take me for?"

She sighed and leaned into him. "The kind of husband who recognizes that I'm capable of doing all that so that I can take care of you."

God had turned her life in a direction she never expected, with a husband more sacrificial than anyone she'd ever known. She reached up and kissed him deeply, hoping all her desires and love showed through. He pulled her close and deepened the kiss. It tasted of salt and anguish and relief.

# EPILOGUE

Robert stood outside of their teepee and inhaled the crisp, clean scent of winter and the Uncompahgre River. The sound of the river rushing and tumbling over rocks battled with the Ute children laughing and chasing each other through the village. The trees with naked branches rattled and swayed in the breeze, and the desert hill jutted with its rocky cliff and flat top on the opposite side of the river. Orange tinted the sky as the sun disappeared over the horizon for another day's end. A few of the elders sat along the riverbank in the waning light, tossing their lines in the water for trout.

Robert loved life here among the Ute people. He shouldn't have worried like he had. When he and Sparrow had returned, the band had been overjoyed for her return. After she'd explained Robert's fight for her survival, they'd accepted him as well. Her arrival had provided the village a small measure of joy in their grief over Chief Ouray's death. Robert was glad Sparrow had been here to help her people in their sadness and fear for the future.

An elder snagged a large trout from the river. The man held up his catch, taunting his friend with it. Robert's deep chuckle burst forth as the fish wiggled violently and jumped from the old man's hands, his gaping mouth a complete contrast to his friend's hearty laughter.

"Robert, love, come on inside." Sparrow's voice beckoned sweetly through the leather wall.

Robert rubbed his hand over a heart full to bursting with peace and love. Though they would most likely be forced onto the reservation and their future was uncertain, he peered at the sky painted pink, orange, and purple and thanked God for redeeming his life, something he seemed to do several times a day. The exasperated call of his wife pushed his mouth into a smile as he ducked into his home—a life worth living promised in the forgiveness of God and the love of Sparrow.

Want more of the Hearts of Roaring Fork Valley series? Pre-order Song of a Determined Heart at a discount direct from the author and get it delivered two weeks before anywhere else.

∽

*Song of a Determined Heart Sneak Peek*

KLARA SORG SWATTED at the hay that tickled her neck. At least she hoped it was straw and not some six- or eight-legged pest she'd unfortunately become accustomed to. She wrinkled her nose at the smell coming from the horse in the stall next to her, the pungency causing her eyes to water. She'd have to remember to muck out the stalls tomorrow since it was obvious Hildebert Müller cared little for his animals.

A shiver skittered down her back, and it wasn't from the freezing cold or the hay. Too bad Hildebert didn't forget about her like he did his animals. He gave her more attention than she wanted. She shivered again and pulled the thin threadbare blanket tighter around her.

How in the world had she gotten here, sleeping in a barn so poorly built you could stand on one side and view the big mountain on the other? Where each night she found a different place to sleep in the small barn so a man nearly twice her age couldn't find her, a married man at that?

*Oh, Vati, why'd you have to drag us here?*

Klara closed her eyes and remembered the day her parents had approached her about their decision to travel west. She'd been playing the piano when they entered the parlor, her father smiling wide and her mother's gold rings clinking together as she wrung her hands.

"Mauschen, we've got some exciting news," her father had said. He'd always called her little mouse, though she was nineteen and far past marrying age. Of course, no one wanted a mute for a wife, so she supposed she'd always be "little mouse." "Klara, we have decided to venture west, to Colorado to be exact."

Colorado needed honest lawyers, and Vati wanted adventure. It didn't matter that Vati was one of the wealthiest men in Ohio. Once he set his heart of something, there was no stopping his determination.

The silver and gold boom popped up new towns left and right. Father had sent out scouts and found that the area called the Roaring Fork Valley showed promise. It wasn't as overrun as Leadville, but also not some place that would turn ghost town overnight. In fact, her father had believed it would be the perfect place to open his attorney office and start a new life.

Klara hadn't wanted a new life full of new people to turn their nose up at her. She begged him to change his mind. Why swap the comforts of the gilded life for they had for an uncouth mining town? When he'd said God might have something good waiting in Colorado for her, she challenged him. God couldn't possibly have anything good in Colorado that she didn't already have in Ohio. She had been right. If only Vati had listened.

Klara stifled the sob that worked up her throat as she thought back to the arduous journey. Her father had hired another "good" German man whose family was also venturing out to Colorado to help them with the move. When they got off the train, the Müllers had been waiting for them.

Three days in, Klara's parents had fallen sick. Bad water. Her mother died that night. Her father followed the next morning, but not before he passed her his small journal that he wrote in daily. His whisper that the Müllers would help her still echoed in her ear. Would she even be able to find their hastily marked grave along the trail?

Klara realized very quickly that the Müller's idea of help was more to their benefit than hers. She rubbed the callouses on her fingers and palms. She'd become less than a scullery maid, not only washing dishes and cleaning the house, but also scrubbing the laundry, gathering eggs, milking the cow, and mucking out stalls. The Müllers insisted that she repay them for their troubles in bringing her to the Roaring Fork Valley and housing her, though Klara figured they'd gotten their pay in her family's belongings they'd either claimed as their own or sold.

Any time Klara spent catching her breath quickly filled with another chore, usually accentuated with a slap on the face or a yank of the hair. She'd been called a stupid, worthless leech so many times, she wondered if it was true. Though Klara figured with the amount of time Maude sat reading her dime novels or buffing her nails, Maude held claim to that title more than Klara. Sure, she didn't know how to cook, but Maude spent such little time each day slapping food together for them that Klara probably could figure out how to do that as well. Klara kept her thoughts to herself since she didn't want yet another chore added to her day.

The dry grass on the other side of the barn wall crunched with the weight of a foot. Klara froze and listened. Another heavy thump set her heart to racing. When the telltale sound of tobacco being spit signaled that Hildebert slunk towards the barn, her meager dinner curdled in her stomach. She buried herself deeper into the hay, curled into a tight ball, and squished her clamped knuckles to her lips.

From the moment her family first got off the train, Hildebert had stared at Klara in ways that had her pulling her shoulders in to hide herself, but his advances hadn't started until a week ago. At first it had been a word in passing about how beautiful she was, "like Maude had once been." Then he had pulled a strand of hair that had fallen out of her bun through his fingers. Two nights ago, he'd started coming to the barn. She'd been able to hide without him finding her, but she wasn't sure how many more hiding spots she'd have before he'd have her cornered.

Now, she burrowed beneath the straw like some rodent hiding from the tom cat. The latch fumbled at the door. Klara squeezed her eyes shut, praying her shivering wouldn't give her away.

"Hildebert." Maude's voice snapped into the cold night air. "What are you doing out there?"

"I was just getting some fresh air. Thought I heard something in the barn." Hildebert's annoyed voice boomed loud within Klara's ears.

"Of course, you heard something, you idiot. The barn is full of animals. Get in here. It's time for bed." Klara wondered if Maude had always talked so harshly to her husband or if his wandering eyes had forced the tone.

Hildebert mumbled as he stomped toward the house. From his angered talking under his breath, Klara was thankful she couldn't understand the words. Her muscles relaxed with the slamming of the house door. Her sigh of relief into the smelly, dusty hay was quickly followed by silent sobs that wracked her body. Her father had been wrong. Colorado offered nothing but heartache and misery.

***Can't wait to know what happens? Preorder from the author and read the adventure two weeks early.***

## ALSO BY SARA BLACKARD

Vestige In Time Series
Vestige of Power
Vestige of Hope
Vestige of Legacy
Vestige of Courage

Stryker Security Force Series
Mission Out of Control
Falling For Zeke
Capturing Sosimo
Celebrating Tina
Crashing Into Jake
Discovering Rafe
Convincing Derrick
Honoring Lena

Alaskan Rebels Series
A Rebel's Heart
A Rebel's Beacon
A Rebel's Promise
A Rebel's Trust

Wild Hearts of Alaska
Wild about Denali

Wild about Violet
Wild about Rory

Hearts of Roaring Fork Valley
Flight of a Wild Heart
Song of a Determined Heart

## ABOUT THE AUTHOR

Sara Blackard has been a writer since she was able to hold a pencil. When she's not crafting wild adventures and sweet romances, she's homeschooling her five children, keeping their off-grid house running, or enjoying the Alaskan lifestyle she and her husband love.

Made in the USA
Coppell, TX
18 February 2024